Hey Mister, Can You Tie My Shoes?

Hey Mister, Can You Tie My Shoes?

ONE MAN'S YEAR AS PLAYGROUND SUPERVISOR AND HIS HUMOROUS TO HILARIOUS OBSERVATIONS FROM THE PLAYGROUND TO THE CAFETERIA AS WELL AS THE CLASSROOM

ROD RATHBUN

TATE PUBLISHING
AND ENTERPRISES, LLC

Published by Tate Publishing & Enterprises, LLC
127 E. Trade Center Terrace | Mustang, Oklahoma 73064 USA
1.888.361.9473 | www.tatepublishing.com

Tate Publishing is committed to excellence in the publishing industry. The company reflects the philosophy established by the founders, based on Psalm 68:11,
"The Lord gave the word and great was the company of those who published it."

Book design copyright © 2014 by Tate Publishing, LLC. All rights reserved.
Cover design by Rtor Maghuyop
Interior Design by Gram Telen
Biography Photo by Riordan Photography

Published in the United States of America

ISBN: 978-1-63449-111-2
Humor / Form / Anecdotes & Quotations
14.10.23

Acknowledgement

I would like to, first and foremost, thank my wife, "Miss Debbie," or just plain Deb, who has been an amazing partner for almost a half century. She keeps me grounded, and is always there to reel me in a little bit, especially when I start to become my own best audience.

Next, I would like to thank my three children, Troy, Tara, and Trent, along with their spouses, Lynn, Mitch, and Cathy, and the incredible eight grandchildren they have blessed us with, and making our lives so meaningful.

Of course, there are numerous friends and relatives who have encouraged me in this endeavor. You all know who you are, but just in case you don't, I'll give you a call later.

I would like to thank the students of St. Michael School for unwittingly supplying me with a treasure trove of things to write about. I would like to thank the teachers and staff that nervously put up with me being there each day, wondering what was going on inside my head, and being transformed into the written word. It is these same people who continue to ask me who will be playing them in the movie version. Hey, you never know!

I would like to thank the principal, Mrs. Davis, who had enough on her plate but still allowed me to document the year.

Lastly, I especially want to thank Sir Paul McCartney in the hope that this book will eventually reach him, and just maybe he will call and thank me for thanking him. After all, it has been a long and winding road, and I am a paperback writer.

—The Playground Supervisor

Contents

1

In the Beginning

It all started with my retirement and those two words: I am bored. Okay, three words if you don't contract *I* and *am*. My wife, known as Miss Debbie, who is and has been a school secretary for thirty-three years, told me about the playground duties and the problems they have on filling the space for a playground supervisor. I thought to myself that maybe that would be a great way to kill some time and feel some worth. First of all, having been in the corporate world for most of my working years, I needed a title. After some considerable thought, I decided on elementary recreational director. I guess they unofficially already had a director, so I had to settle for supervisor. Okay, that part was behind me. Now what I didn't expect: all the paperwork and, of course, the hair follicle samples. Being "follically" challenged, I opted for the chest hair removal. I know I must have signed my name on enough papers to begin the process of forming a new country. Next was the mandatory movie on how to deal with blood and vomit. This was a pretty disgusting movie. I only hope no one bleeds. I have always had two words when it came to dealing with such substances:I don't". When it came to my own kids, I changed fewer diapers than the number of underwear worn by the Kardashian girls.

Okay, first day of school. Talk about scary and intimidating. I have dealt with corporate executives who didn't cause me to quiver as much as 144 loud and demanding prepubescent school kids. Also cute—did I mention cute? I thought I would start the year out with high-fives to the kindergarteners. I didn't continue this on with the first graders because of the broken blood vessel in my hand. Gee, those kids high-five hard. There is always that one kid you know right away you never—and I mean never—turn your back on. In this case his name was Raymond, but in order to protect his privacy, I will refer to him as Bob. Bob's first words to me after the high five were, "Hey, mister, I got a girlfriend." Okay, that's going to be interesting to track over the years.

My next duty was executing the task of getting all these children from point A to point B with a tray full of food. You would think—by the way they negotiated this movement—that they were walking on a tightrope strung above the Grand Canyon. In many cases, the laws of physics were broken. How is it possible for a Hello Kitty canister not to fall off the tray while being carried at a seventy degree angle? Did I mention that this is a Catholic school? Obviously there is a divine intervention going on here.

Okay, lunch is over and no obvious catastrophes, so it is time to line up and go outside. I know that after a filling meal, my first thought is to take a nice little nap, burp a little, and enjoy a little piece and quiet. Not so with the little ones. They don't nap, and they don't enjoy a little peace and quiet—but they do burp. There is enough energy displayed on that playground to power a spaceship from here to the moon. My one main thought is for no one to get hurt, and yes, of course, having as many kids at the end of the play period that I had at the beginning of it.

At the time of this, my first playground duty, it is toward the end of August. My clothes are saturated and stuck to places I didn't even know I had, and the sun is causing my eyes to glue shut. It is at this point when prayer crosses one's lips. Please, Lord, let that bell that ends recess ring. I can see that there is one minute left to go. Thirty seconds, ten seconds, and then finally, "Line up! Time to go in!" Now I can go home. Not so fast. There is the part of chasing down and account for every ball and jump rope and any other item that was being played with on the grounds. As you would figure, we came up short. A further investigation revealed that some of the items found their way within a two-block area. "Don't anybody move. I'll go get them." Okay, everything accounted for. Now l can go home.

By now your body is telling you that evening is approaching, and it is time for that relaxing and well-deserved beer. Unbelievably it is only 12:30 p.m. Well, maybe just a few minutes of nap time. Oops, it's 4:30 p.m., and I hear my wife pulling into the garage. Where did that afternoon go? Guess what? I get to do this again tomorrow.

2

I Was Just Joking

Yes, I did go back. It is startling to witness the transformation in just a few short days from those scared young children who are crying and missing their moms to the loud, brave, and overly energetic kids who, from their over exuberance, resort to name calling and crotch punching. And then there was the sticking out of the tongue. Okay, I know I shouldn't have done it, but they made me mad.

I realized that what was popular fifty years ago may not be today. Pickles seemed to be the most popular item on the menu on this particular day. As my duties included serving this item, I felt that it was funny and clever to tell the kids going through the line that these popular pickles were picked by Peter Piper. I know that in the original the main item was peppers, but I thought just stringing together a bunch of P words would be funny. Needless to say, on my first attempt at standup comedy, I fell flat on my face. However, I know I will try again when the cafeteria serves seashells.

It was a casual day today, so I wore a T-shirt that I have been saving for three years. I bought it at a Paul McCartney concert but have just been waiting for the right occasion to wear it. The reactions were many. "I like your shirt." "Who's that guy?" "Does he play for Quiet Riot?" "What's a Beatle?" Yes, I feel old.

As I once again tried to regain my youth, I thought it would be a good idea to tell a little joke. Keep in mind that the vast majority of jokes that come out of my mouth are not suitable for the young or, in many cases, the prudish. My worst audience is Miss Debbie, who finds no humor in most of my attempts at comedy. She says it is because she has heard the jokes several hundreds of times and knows what the punch line is. Anyway my joke today to the kindergarten kids was the following: What is a pirate's favorite letter? The answer is *rrrrrr*. This is funny to a five-year-old. Of course, no matter what age a person is, there is still that desire to one up the joke teller with their own on the spot joke. Maggie then piped in with, "What do you get when a pig knows karate?" The answer is a pork chop. Okay, she got me. Miss Debbie even laughed at that one. Still more jokes were coming. I guess after absorbing my joke, Kevin decided that his was funnier. What are sunglasses favorite letter? Could it be *rrrrrr*? No Kevin had another take on it and decided that *eeeee* would be funnier. I don't get it. Of course, this went on for most of the lunch hour and caused me to be mildly reprimanded by the other supervisor for distracting the kids from their lunch. I have to admit that several lunches got tossed today, but if they think that is bad, wait 'til tomorrow when I perform the magic show.

Well, it finally happened. There was an injury on the playground—me. I took a hundred mile an hour soccer ball between the shoulder blades. Well, it felt like one hundred miles an hour. As I recovered to replace the air back into my collapsed lungs and tears welled up in my eyes, I recalled that famous saying, "There's no crying in playground supervising."

Now for the tip of the day: I really don't know if chocolate milk that comes in the small cardboard containers has to be shaken, but what I do know is that it should not be shaken after it has been opened. Enough said on that subject.

Today was not the kid's favorite meal, macaroni and cheese, broccoli, and carrots. I witnessed for the first time in my life what an interesting color these food groups make when mixed together. Kids love to emulate mixologists when it comes to items on their plates that they choose not to eat; however, I am still puzzled by the color when red catsup, yellow mustard, and chocolate milk combined on one of the student's plate became a lovely shade of brown almost reminiscent of what a new parent finds in a baby's diaper. Yummy.

3

Forty-four Years Ago

I probably should have mentioned that I actually taught at this school some forty-four years ago, when I was starting out in the work force. At the time, my dad was very skeptical of my skills as a teacher, and as time went on, he would closely monitor my actions. I held this seventh grade teaching profession for three years; and as the coming years came and passed, my dad would always ask me about the students whose lives I affected. I told him that I have kept in touch with many of them even to the point of having a twenty-year grade school reunion. My former students have become teachers, doctors, judges, lawyers, nuclear power plant supervisors, dental hygienists or whatever you call them (people who assist dentists), business owners, a slew of other reputable occupations, and one kid wanted by the FBI—wait a minute, how did he get in there? Anyway my dad would gleam with pride over the years as I told him about the success my former students had achieved and would boast to his friends about his son the teacher, the molder of character, the designer of minds, the creator of ideas, and then privately would take me aside and say, "Well, son, there's another one you didn't hurt."

4

Just Deal with It

Today when I arrived at the cafeteria, I first checked the board to see what was being served. The main entrée for today was Italian dunkers and since I have never heard of the term, I right away assumed that two hairy Italian gentlemen by the names Guido and Giuseppe had volunteered their services for a dunk tank. To my surprise, that was not the case. As it turns out, Italian dunkers appear to be bread sticks that you dunk in chili. Actually, the kids seemed to like it. My thoughts on future meals that are guaranteed to be a hit would be things like Superman Sausage, Batman Borscht, and Spiderman Spaghetti. I am not sure how Barbie beef tips would go over with the boys though.

It was very boring for me today since no condiments were required for me to put on the kids' trays. I did have to break up two second graders standing in line who were attempting to kick each other in the "privates." It was a he said, she said situation. She said, "He tried to kick me in the privates." He said, "She tried to kick me in the two privates." I settled this by asking them which one wanted to go back to first grade. There were no volunteers, so this issue was laid to rest. For now.

Out on the playground saw the usual run, catch, kick (which is against the rules), and other activities. It was 12:29, one minute to go before end of recess—and wouldn't you know it, we have a mishap. A first grader falls and scrapes his knee, hand, and elbow. I immediately attended to the situation and with much sensitivity said, "Couldn't you have waited just one more minute?" "Okay, let's go to the office." I found out that there is paperwork for everything. Let's see…What happened, how did it happen, who was involved, did anyone else witness the incident? There was a sign of relief finding out that everything was fine and most likely there will be no lawsuit. My hour for today ended up being ninety minutes. There is nothing like a little time and a half over time. Yeah right.

Another day, another dollar. Here we go again. Today I committed the cardinal sin of condiments. "Hey, mister, can I have some catsup on my tenderloin?" "Sure, Brady," I said. I am priding myself on learning all of the kid's first names. "My name is not Brady." Oh, back to the yearbook. "Okay kid, not a problem." I must have been rattled or something because the catsup came out yellow. "Hey, that's mustard. I hate mustard!" You would have thought that I just bombed Syria without seeking congressional approval. Well, I don't know how much I cost the cafeteria today, but you learn really fast that you don't tell a first grader to just "deal with it."

For some reason, these kids don't know how to tie their shoes. They have tiny little feet, with tiny little shoes, that have a tiny light that lights up, and the shoelaces are four feet long. How in God's name are you supposed to tie those things without three feet of laced bow flopping in the wind as they run? Where is Velcro when you need it?

Another little boy in first grade lost a tooth today. I am going to say that his name is Jeremy, but I still question my ability to remember names. I noticed he had his fist in his mouth, and when I asked him what he was doing, he said, "I ga a woose toof." Now I was trained in many aspects of playground supervising but learning a language that does not exist was not one of them, yet my cognitive thinking brought me to the conclusion that he had a loose tooth. I told him that it would probably be better if he worked on it at home tonight. Not gonna happen. Within two minutes, we had a little boy with shaking fingers holding number 21 tooth. I learned the numbering system from finally going to the dentist. In my day that would be twenty five cents coming from the tooth fairy but a random survey indicated that we might be looking at five dollars. Boy, I was born way too soon. Stay tuned for more exciting adventures. Yep, it was five dollars.

5

Boys Will Be Boys and So Will Girls

Rumor has it (allegedly, you have to say *allegedly* in this ridiculous day and age of political correctness) that the kindergarten girls have been chasing the boys to get a kiss. Boy, have times changed. In my day, it was the boys who chased the girls to get a kiss. After much thought and consideration, it became very clear to me. We as boys had guidance back in those days that made us boys. Girls were sugar and spice and everything nice, and boys were snips and snails and puppy dog tails. I am not sure what a snip is, but I am sure it is manly. However, the biggest influence on us boys came from…Georgie Porgie, pudding and pie, kissed the girls and made them cry. When the girls came out to play, Georgie Porgie ran away. Okay, let's analyze this. First of all, I am not fond of the name Georgie Porgie, It should have been Rocco Socco or Sammy Whammy or something like that. Now let's get to the pudding and pie part. Back then pudding and pie was our main lunch staple, so who could blame those sugar high boys running around wanting to get a kiss? In today's society, we have Michelle Obama who has introduced a diet of cardboard and flavorless pap that is supposed to energize today's young men. Then we have kissed the girls and made them cry. Well, I do have to admit that at five years old, my kissing technique was not that good, so I can understand the crying part. Finally, when the girls came out to play, Georgie Pordgie ran away. Of course, we ran away because the principal was looking for us, and we knew that we were in big trouble. But kissing back then was like salmon swimming upstream to spawn. You knew the eventual consequences, but it still didn't stop you.

As I sit here writing this, my thoughts have reverted back to my classmates of yore (I thought I would add a little Shakespeare here to class this up a little). Wouldn't it be nice to get those girls that I went to kindergarten with to chase me for a kiss? After a little research, I realized that out of the twelve girls that I went to school with, three are dead, four have orthopedic shoes and get around on a walker, two of them I didn't want to kiss back then (and I really don't want to kiss now) and the remaining three don't even remember kindergarten, let alone me.

6

Memories Are Made of This

After three weeks of observation, I remain really confused. My focus on this chapter is going to concentrate on the principal and kitchen help. Why do today's principals look like they should be on the cover of *Vanity Fair* or *Cosmopolitan* magazine? In my day, the principal looked like the twin sister of the wicked witch of the west. Her name was Miss Schiffer, and I do mean Miss. If she weighed seventy pounds, I would be surprised. I don't really remember if she had a basket on the back of her bicycle, but at the end of the day, I can recall saying, "There's no place like home." I lived four blocks from the grade school that I went to for my entire elementary years. I vividly remember for the longest time that my dog Smokey (his real name) would follow me to school each day and be there waiting for me six hours later. I really miss that dog. No, not Miss Schiffer, Smokey. The only loyalty you will find like that today is when your relatives stick by you waiting for you to cash in your winning lottery ticket at the local 7Eleven.

I vividly remember my cafeteria in grade school. Our cafeteria cooks had names like Blanche, Zelda, Mavis, and Maude. They had big black hairnets that came together like a sniper's target in the middle of their forehead. I have a visual of long armpit hairs sticking out of their short sleeved uniforms as they ladled wilted spinach laced with vinegar on to my tray. The aroma of body odor continues to haunt me to this day every time I am within thirty feet of chicken noodle soup. I still believe that my apple sauce had remnants of cigarette ashes in it. We usually sat in the same location on tables that pulled out of the wall. I specifically remember sitting in the same place each day because I would stick to the same grape jelly dropping. I still am convinced that the gravy was mixed with Elmer's glue to make it go farther.

Today's cooks are assisted by moms and dads who appear to be no more than two years out of eighth grade and searching for a prom dress or tux. You can see the pride in their faces along with the fear in their eyes as their little ones come through the lunch line. It is not until the tray gets to the table without incident when the parent takes that breath and you can see the color return back to their face. Mothers have been observed bringing their younger children to the cafeteria. One mom in particular had her six-month-old daughter strapped to her back for the entire fifty minutes while scooping out peaches. I think I would have placed the kid on one of those heavy duty hooks where they hang the large pots and pans. But that's just me.

7

I Don't Think So

Well, today was different to say the least. I was asked to concentrate my time with the preschoolers. They can be really cute and adorable…for about two minutes, and then obnoxiousness (Gee, I never remember spelling that word before) sets in, or it may be that my patience gave out. Right in the middle of lunch, one of the preschoolers who speaks very little English and will remain nameless (for documentation purposes, we will call him Ricky), decides that he had to go to the *baño*. For you gringos out there, that means bathroom. Now I am not one who cares to assume things, but in this particular case, I did assume that he needed to go number one. As I placed him in front of the urinal, he got this weird look on his face. Here I am trying to keep the door ajar with my foot and instructing him to do what he had to do. I briefly turned to talk to a teacher passing by, and then as I refocused my attention back to Ricky, I noticed that he was sitting in the urinal speaking words that were foreign to me. It was then that the language barrier was no longer an obstacle. I kept thinking that I did not sign up for this. I then directed him to the correct porcelain fixture and verbally from a distance gave him the instructions compatible with that area of the restroom. In a couple of minutes, Ricky emerged from the stall and handed me a wad of toilet paper thinking that I had the supervisory skills needed to clean up in aisle six. Sorry, kid, it ain't gonna happen. I was trained on blood and vomit but not *caca*. You are on your own. Well, I finally got him back to his table as three other boys did their impression of Donald Trump and told me that I was fired. Honestly, taking these kids to the bathroom is one job I really don't mind being fired from. *Adios, amigos!*

I found out today from the preschool teacher that the preschoolers have a jar in their room and every time someone does something good, they get to put a marble in it and when the jar gets full, they get a surprise. I told her that I am going to get a jar and put it in my house and every time my wife does something good, I will put a marble in it. I pretty much figured I will not be needing very many marbles.

8

Who Is That Guy?

Today I noticed that the preschoolers and kindergarten kids pretty much refer to me as "Hey you." I always know that my services are immediately needed when I hear those words. "Hey, you, can you open my milk"? "Hey, you, I forgot a napkin". "Hey, you what's your name "? I am always ready to help. Then it became clear to me that the next three grades or so refer to me as sir. "Sir, are you going to be here all year?" "Sir, can we go and get seconds?" We then get to the middle grade students who are a little bit sarcastic. They refer to you as mister. "Hey, Mister, come here." As I obediently stop what I am doing and cross the room, I finally arrive at the destination only to hear "Never mind." Now we get to the older kids. First of all, they don't really need your help opening milk or other food products; however, there is some sort of sneakiness to them, and for that reason, they don't call you by any name. I guess they figure that the less attention they draw to themselves, the better it is for them. You sometimes get a feeling that there is some sort of covert operation going on. Low murmurs become total silence as you near their table. They have a camaraderie of sorts being in that early teen world where they know that everyone is against them. Sort of a misery loves company mentality. Now it is totally different in the early grades where Logan will rat out Carson for an Oreo cookie. They will go for each other's throats at the drop of a pin. If you look at somebody and it happens to be the wrong time of the day, you are at risk of having your eyes poked out. It is amazing how these kids seem to know the most vulnerable parts of the body without being taught, but the nice thing about these brutal pugilistic bouts is that these same two young men are best friends in about three minutes. If only our world leaders could observe and emulate these little guys.

Today out on the playground we had a good news, bad news, good news, bad news, good news situation. First the good news: Kayla came to school in a nice, spotless, clean uniform skirt. Now the bad news: Kayla got some white blots of something all over her nice, clean skirt. Now the good news: We should be able to clean it. Now the bad news: I think it is bird poop. Now the good news: Nope, it is ranch dressing from today's lunch. I learned today that it is not a good idea to touch it, let alone taste it until you really know what it is that you are dealing with. Luckily it was not a caustic germ warfare substance.

9

You Make Me Sick

When I was asked to take over the supervision of the preschoolers on Tuesday and Thursday, I was not aware of two things. First, more food gets left on the floor than actually enters their stomachs, and secondly, that look they can give you when they are not real pleased at being disciplined causes you to question your ability to be the one in control. It is a big mistake to confuse cuteness with sinister. There were times today when I chose to give myself a time out just so I could be separated from them. The headcount was fifteen, and with them running in every different direction, it is next to impossible to get a reliable total. I think I could be more accurate counting bees being excavated from their hive. The nice thing about watching the preschoolers is—let me come back to that at a later date, possibly graduation day. Preschool can have as many as three adults in the classroom. All of the other classes have one. That should tell you something. Your first thought would be that they need more attention because of being young, but after further evaluation, I am certain that it is for the protection of the teachers. Lions, tigers, and bears (oh my) can appear docile and tame, but the minute you turn your back and assume things are safe, it can be all over for you.

Today brought up new fears for me since I am a hardcore, card-carrying, germaphobic, but only if that card has been thoroughly sanitized. I observed one of the youngsters eating lunch with that glistening stream of milky white, crusty mucus coming out of his left nostril. These are also the type of kids who insist on touching you. It seems that no matter how many napkins you give them, their hands are always wet and sticky. And then there was sweet little Taylor who called me over to tell me something. As I got closer to hear that tiny voice, I could feel her breath wash over my face and then those words came out, "I got a cold." I am not sure at this point how I will get through the winter flu season. A person can only hold their breath for so long, and you know that no matter how careful you are, there is always that one time or maybe two times—okay, a couple dozen times—that for one reason or another, you stick your finger in your nose and all those germs start spreading like Miley Cyrus at a photo shoot.

10

Don't Get Personal

Little kids for some reason seem to be very interested in my personal life, especially since I let it be known that Miss Debbie, the secretary, is my wife. One little girl today wanted to know how we met, who had a crush on who, how long did we date. This particular seven-year-old was also deeply troubled and quite concerned over her fourteen-year-old brother's inability to get a girlfriend. She proceeded to tell me that she is afraid that he has reached a point in his life where it is too late for him to get anybody. As I began to assure her that things have a way of working out, it occurred to me that before I get too involved, I should probably refer this case to Dr. Phil.

My next patient shared with me how difficult it is to remove sand from your skin that you get from the beaches of Hawaii. I was told that you have to pick off each grain one by one. I can't relate to that one since Hawaii has never been one of my ports of call.

Thinking that my office calls were done for the day, Patient Number 3 tells me that her favorite smell is rare steak on the grill. Now this patient I can sympathize with. Each kid in his or her way has the most important thing to tell you. I am happy to be that listening ear. The only problem with that though is that it can be quite noisy in the lunch room, and you have to get closer to actually hear what those little voices are saying and when you do, spittle and food particles find their way into your ear canal, causing a moment of awkward deafness and that old familiar feeling of a wet willy. So now when I don't hear what they are saying to me, I just nod my head yes, and if I don't get the reaction from them that I think I should be getting, I then nod my head no and usually one of those responses is the right one.

It is quite interesting to try and decipher what some of these kids are thinking and trying to convey. One little girl was overheard saying that her mother was going to have a baby any day and it was going to be a vegetarian. Translation: my mom is pregnant and the child will be born by caesarean section. A second little girl was so excited about her revelation that Jesus and God are brothers. Translation: I was not paying attention during religion class. I felt bad for her since everyone knows that Jesus and God are cousins on their father's side.

I kind of got a compliment today. I was told by a preschooler that he liked my hair. That was the compliment. I asked him why he would say that, and he said because it reminded him of a kneepad. I am not sure where to go from there on that one.

Today we had pepperoni pizza. The pepperoni was sprinkled on in little pieces. One little girl who apparently doesn't like pepperoni proceeded to methodically pick off every tiny last bit of it with the precision of a diamond cutter until a small pile was accumulating in a separate tray division. With more due diligence and determination than a bomb diffuser, she completed her task. It was a thing of beauty to observe. One problem, lunch is over, and it is time to go out for recess and a pepperoni-less pizza now sits idle and untouched on the tray.

11

You Bug Me

As I was patrolling the playground area, I noticed two young kindergarten lads crouched together over in the corner, apparently up to something devious. As I approached unnoticed, it became clear that they were in the process of harnessing as many insects as they could for the sole purpose of causing a reaction from the girls. Fortunately, I was able to step in and put this potential terrorist action to rest. In doing so, my mind found its way back to 1964 when I was a sophomore in high school biology class. Back then I did not have the years of experience that I have today. Short cuts were part of my daily regimen. We were required to have an insect collection, which is a time-consuming project. As was accustomed for me back in those days, I waited for the last minute. We were required to have a specific number of insect species, and I was lacking a couple. I captured a spider, put him in his eternal sleep, labeled him—or her, not sure which because I didn't look that closely—and pinned it inside the cigar box. A friend then told me that spiders are not insects because they have eight legs. Well, I knew he was smarter than me because he told me. It is very important to be able to think on your feet and adapt, so I pulled off two legs, bringing it to a total of six. That makes it an insect, right? Maybe the teacher wouldn't notice. Okay, that crisis averted. Now I needed a grasshopper to complete the project. I was successful in the capture and took him or her into the house for the euthanasia. Protocol calls for the victim to be put in a jar with a cotton ball soaked in formaldehyde until death sets in. As luck would have it, no formaldehyde in the house. I made the bold decision to drown the poor guy or gal in the sink. After several minutes, I took the poor thing out, labeled it, and pierced it with a pin where it was then stuck in the cigar box, thus completing my insect biology project.

The next day being Monday is usually the worst day of the week to double-check anything. I was running late, grabbed my project, and proceeded on to school. Biology was my first class of the day. I proudly presented the box to the instructor and took my seat with the rest of the class. What I am about to tell you is not for the faint of heart, especially mine. The teacher who was affectionately known as "Buggie" selected mine as the first one to open. To my horror and dismay, apparently divine intervention stepped in and brought my grasshopper back to life. He or she pulled loose from the mounting and was spinning around inside the box with this pin impaled in it sort of like a Milton Bradley game. It must have gotten a little hungry and decided to enjoy the buffet surrounding it and ate four and a half of my other bugs. The only thing at this point that was not in doubt was the grade that I was going to get on the project. I later found out that my project was displayed in each class for the rest of the day as a model of how not to complete a Biology insect collection project. Thank God for the sex education part of biology where I obtained an A grade to offset the F.

Reality has now set in, and my time travels bring me back to present day. As the glaze leaves my eyes and sweat beads have accumulated on my forehead, I see these two young boys standing before me, holding their insect treasures. If only they would have been my friends back then, I maybe would have gotten a D. Okay, boys, wrap it, put those things down and line up to go inside, and you should probably wash your hands.

12

I Can't Believe You Just Did That

After a few weeks of observation, I have come to the educated conclusion that the Appalachian coal miners come out of the mines after a ten-hour shift cleaner than the preschoolers do after a twenty-minute lunch. The puzzling thing is that their plates appear untouched. They don't like carrots, they don't like this particular type of macaroni and cheese, and they don't like the strawberry tarts. But the mystery remains: how did they get so soiled? Not only are their shirts spotted, but it also seems they have been sitting on their food. I have been watching closely thinking that with this being a Catholic school maybe some of these spots might be in the image of a holy icon, but after close examination, nope, they are just spots. Should any future markings appear to be divine in nature, you can be rest assured that I will follow up another book titled *See Spot Run* or *Angels in My Broccoli*.

Out on the playground with today's political correctness, the kids are not allowed to play dodge ball. I grew up on dodge ball, and it is a blast. The object of the game is to hit your opponent with a ball to knock him or her out of the competition. If you are accurate with your throw, they are eliminated. If you are hit with a ball, then you are gone. If they catch the ball, then you have been eliminated. If you catch the ball, then they are out of the game. It is very simple and lots of fun. I guess some congressional committee somewhere decided that this is demeaning and could lead to a lifetime of self-degradation and a poor self-image to those who lose and therefore should not be played. This has been explained to the children that playing dodge ball will under no circumstances be tolerated; however, they do manage to play dodge bean bags, dodge Frisbee, and dodge jump rope. Oh yeah, I forgot to mention they also play dodge ball.

Also, today out on the grounds I felt it was necessary to grab the preschooler's attention. I once heard that the attention span of a fish is about two seconds. With four- and five-year-old kids, it is less than that. I came up with the idea to see how many of them could walk the yellow painted strip that separates the cars in the parking lot without stepping outside of it. It is never too early to teach these kids about field sobriety. They all did pretty well, so we advanced on to standing on one foot and alternating their index fingers to their nose. This is where I lost them, but I am pretty sure that I held their attention for longer than two seconds.

Hey Mister, Can You Tie My Shoes?

Problem solving seems to be my main focus out on the playground. To give you an idea as to the challenges I encounter, I am prepared to relate two such incidents that occurred within a ten minute period of time. First there was sweet little Kenna. This little girl is capable of eating any type of food source with just the tips of her right forefinger and thumb. After completely finishing her meal, there really is no need for the use of a napkin, but she methodically uses it anyway to wipe away any residual pieces of food particles. It is after observing her dining habits that makes it impossible for me to comprehend what happened out on the playground. As Kenna approached me, I could see her hand clinched tightly. She proceeded to inform me that she had found something out on the playground. I reached out my hand, palm upward, to accept the object that this sweet little girl wanted to entrust in my care. As her hand slowly opened, the object carefully dropped onto my outstretched hand. It took a few seconds before the image registered to my brain. I guess there are worse items out there, but realizing I was holding a freshly discarded used Band-Aid was about as much as I could take. To a person with germ phobias, this is just about the holy grail of all objects that are not to be touched, except for maybe used underwear and a saliva-soaked cough drop. After a quick trip to the restroom—well, maybe not that quick—and completely depleting the soap dispenser, I guess I was ready to go back out to the battle ground to complete my obligation as playground supervisor.

It is clear to me that I have to be a supervisor, policeman, psychologist, friend, a confidant, a medical assistant, and overall good guy. I am not sure which hat I had to wear when this serene-looking little kindergarten girl came over and informed me that she had just heard a bad word from one of the older kids. I am thinking to myself that I may have to call in reinforcements on this matter. I asked her what that word might be and in those sweet, little, innocent eyes looking straight into mine, she revealed to me that the horrible word was…alcoholic. I told her that I would handle the situation and thanked her for calling it to my attention. I think I reacted in the right way. After all, if you look alcoholic up in the dictionary, it is accompanied by a picture of a playground supervisor. I just can't wait to go home and have a drink, or maybe more than one. Okay, several.

13

Seriously

I would like to take a minute to say something a little serious... serious. Sorry, I couldn't help myself.

14

Love Is in the Air

Hamburgers seem to be the kid's favorite lunch meal at the school. There are more ways to dispense condiments than you can imagine. First, there is the catsup on the burger, there is catsup on the bun, and there is catsup on the side for dipping. The few brave souls go for the combination catsup and mustard and pickles. As far as French fries are concerned, some want it on the fries while others prefer it away from the fries. With the preschoolers, we are fortunate to have the teacher and assistant help in getting the kids settled. The teachers then abandon us to go for their well-deserved private time. The daily ritual includes the children telling the teachers that they love them. "I love you, Miss So and So." Today I finally asked them why they never tell me that they love me. Luke said that it was because I was a guy, and guys can't marry guys. Normally, I would have agreed with him, but as fast as things are changing in today's society, I felt it was a good time to move to another table and not bring Elton John into the conversation. Actually the L word in my way of thinking is a very difficult four-letter word to say. It can mean that you would love to get rid of this gassy feeling. I would love to get my sinus cleared up. I would love to cure my foot fungus, or I would really love to get rid of this rectal itch. With these kids, it means something else, and it is a word that will probably cost them a lot of money down the road.

I decided to stop at the third grade table to see how things were going. Again, the sound of romance was in the air. One young lady was mortified that the boy sitting next to her wanted to be her boyfriend. I believe her exact words were, "He makes me want to vomit." She insisted that she liked him as a friend but not a boyfriend. After much embarrassment, I asked her if she actually had a boyfriend. She stated that there is one boy that she likes who goes to another school and that he is her boyfriend. A third grade girl sitting across from her piped in that her brother has a boyfriend. Huh?! I was confused. It was time to move on.

Out on the playground, a kindergarten girl reported to me that she had an injury. Louis Pasteur could not have found the injury with his microscope. As I removed my cell phone, I told the young girl that I would call an ambulance and that I knew a doctor who specialized in these types of injuries, and if all went well, she would be up and around in two or three weeks. All of a sudden, the injury had gone away, and it was obvious that my career as a faith healer was ready to begin. Another young girl reported to me the theft of a jump rope by two other girls that she was going to use. I felt this was my opportunity to use my crime solving skills. I pulled out the trusty cell phone and told her I would call the police. I guess she had second thoughts on filing charges, so I didn't make the call. When you are so instrumental in bringing these crisis situations to an immediate and safe conclusion, you start thinking of yourself as having superhuman powers and basking in the glow of knowing that the world is a better place because you are in it, and it is then when reality sets in and you are back home and Miss Debbie says, "Take the garbage out, you idiot."

15

They Were Kids Too

As I was walking around the cafeteria today, I was struck by the self-imposed question as to who will these young kids become? What does life have in store for them? I am convinced that the cafeteria years are some of the most influential in a child's life. Everybody has gone through the cafeteria line at some time or another. The friends you make and the conversations you have and just the overall experience of eating and socializing together forms the structure of who you are and who you will become. For instance, a young Barack Obama was a student in Indonesia and went to the cafeteria every day with his Karl Marx logo lunchbox. He would confront the cooks and say, "The food is good, but you can do better. The question is, do you have the strength and determination to change? I am bothered by those folks over there in the eighth grade. They got more chicken nuggets than the folks in first and second grade. We gotta do something about that. We need to spread the nuggets around more equally."

It was reported that a young Ozzie Osbourne when going through the line said, "I I I I I I I I I want a —— live chicken so I can eat his —— head off and I I I I I I I I I am not *Sharon* it with anybody."

A quiet and shy Elvis would sit by himself and not talk to anybody, and then one day he got up and went over to the cook and said, "I got some catsup on my blue suede shoes, and I'm all shook up cause when I go back in the ghetto my mama's gonna be mad at me, but the food was Amazing, Grace. I especially loved my tenders. Thank you, Thank you very much."

Norma Jean Baker, a.k.a Marilyn Monroe, was also a quiet, shy little girl who had to be brought out of her shell. One day the playground supervisor went up to her and asked her how her soup was. She was quoted as saying, "It was very, very, very good, but a little cold and as you know Some Like It Hot."

Also, we cannot forget that famous blonde actress Reese something or another who used to eat everything with her fork and now she eats everything with her spoon, but I will be damned if I can remember her name.

And then there was that poor little Joan of Arc who was last in line and with the food running out she said, "I'm sorry I am late, I got tied up I'll take the Burnt Steak."

Okay, I am not too sure of the quotes being exact, but it could have happened. Maybe.

16

In My Shoes

On several occasions during the noon hour, we are assisted by the teachers in getting the kids settled down and cooperative. Not enough can be said about these brave souls who have dedicated their lives in furthering a child's education and growth. In one particular teacher, you can see the years of hard work and struggle in every wrinkle on her face. The bags under her eyes are a testament to her devotion and the long hours she has faced in building her craft, and her bones creek from the nonstop attention given to each and every student under her tutelage. I think she will be twenty-two next month.

This was a school that several years ago had a staff of nuns as their teaching force. They were bundled up in their habits with just the tip of their nose poking through. We will never know how they survived those ninety- to one hundred-degree days with no air condition. Their patience had to have reached the limit of human endurance. I think we can believe those stories about the ruler. Kids back then had to be petrified as to the changing mood of the women in black.

Once again this brings me back to my own experiences as a youngster in grade school and the teachers back then. One female gym teacher who fit that stereotype to a tee probably had enough skeletons in her closet to be able to have Halloween every day of the year. We as young boys striving to cross over into that realm of manhood were intimidated by her masculinity. However, there was an air of attraction that to this day cannot be grasped. Popeye had Olive Oyle, and we had the gym teacher.

We had a class called industrial arts, which allowed us to work with tools. Yes, we were able to use real tools to build things back then, and I don't remember anybody cutting off any important protrusions. As much fun as this class was, there was one thing that is troubling to this day. Hanging on the wall was a large paddle with a hole in the middle of it that was used to swat a misbehaving lad on the backside. The hole in the middle had the effect of sucking in the fleshy part to what was being smacked. I think the real problem that we had is that we were instructed to make this paddle as a class project knowing that it was most likely going to find its mark on us. It is kind of freaky, now that you think of it.

Along with industrial arts came regular art class. Where else can you make beautiful jewelry for your mother out of a cork, some pins, and sequin beads? I can still remember to this day as my mom would dress up and put on those beautiful cork earrings and head out the door for her glamorous evening. I stood there proudly saying to myself, "I made those." It wasn't until several years later that I found out she switched them in the car. If only she would have told me…I could have used them to go fishing.

Back in those days, one of my best friends just happened to be the son of my seventh grade teacher. You would think that would have given me a one up on everyone else in the class, but according to my report card, that was not the case. On one particular weekend night, I was invited to stay overnight. This was a typical sleep over that thousands of kids have each week, but you must remember this was my teacher's house. As the early morning sun started to flood the bedroom with its luster and my eyes breaking from the crust left behind from my deep slumber, I caught a vision brief as it was of my seventh grade teacher walking in the room without the benefit of makeup and a ragged and tattered nightgown draped around her. I have tried for years to get this vision out of my mind, but the image is as strong as a fart in a Coke bottle. I know because I've tried it.

17

Loaded and Locked

Out on the playground today, everything seemed to be going pretty smoothly. I was told that the preschoolers were only one marble away from that coveted surprise which no one seemed to have any idea as to what that surprise was. My marble jar at home remains empty, but that's another series of books. Anyway, as I mentioned in an earlier chapter, a student whom we know as Ricky had bathroom issues, which caused much distress for this playground supervisor. Ricky had to once again use the facilities, so you can imagine my distress associated with this function. As I relayed to the other supervisor where I was about to go and with whom, she yelled back for me not to leave her any longer than I had to. I know the panic going through her body was real and not imagined.

Apparently, Ricky must have some kind of an incontinence problem associated with men over seventy, but he is only four. Off we went, and here he was ten yards ahead of me, which is hard for anyone to do when they are taking three-inch steps while holding on to that part of the body that was aching to be relieved. Thankfully we made it in time, and with several past trips to this particular facility, Ricky knew what was expected and where to go. As he closed the door on the stall, I quickly remembered my Spanish and alertly said, "Peese don't luke de dor." Too late, he luked de dor. After finishing what sounded like Niagara Falls springing a leak, Ricky yelled out, "Can't open door." "Ricky, just do what you did when you locked it but do it the opposite way," to which he replied, "Que?" There is probably an eight-inch space between the bottom of the door and the floor. I could always crawl under there and rescue him, but my germ phobia kicked in and that wasn't going to happen. I could see his little feet under the door, and after much coaxing, I was able to get him to stick a foot out so I could pull him to safety. Ricky has been rescued and once again I am a hero; however, the door was still locked and no one was in there. Ricky bolted out of the bathroom and was off faster than a prom dress. When I couldn't find him, I asked one of the students if he saw where Ricky went, to which he replied, "Yep, he's over there in the green shirt." Thanks, kid. Wait a minute. This is a Catholic school. They wear uniforms, and they all have green shirts.

Safely returning to the playground area, I immediately summoned someone who was familiar with the locking mechanism, and was small enough to squeeze under the door and had no concern toward germ warfare. Thank God for first graders.

I reported my experience to the preschool teacher thinking that this was a once-in-a lifetime happening with the intention of preventing any such occurrence transpiring again. Her response to me was, "Oh yeah, he did that this morning."

18

Let There Be Light

Today brought me to my knees. Normally, I am a very easygoing guy. I am one of those individuals who just loves a laidback rainy day. The sound of the rain hitting the ground, the feel of rain drops caressing your forehead, and the smell permeating though your nostrils from wet, freshly cut grass is something really special. After today, I hope it never rains again. When you have rain, you have noon hour indoors. Since I was in charge of the smaller children, we had the old small gym. I played basketball in this gym some fifty-five years ago. I coached basketball in this gym when I was a teacher here and know each and every nook and cranny that this facility has to offer. When I got there after lunch, I was concerned as to the dim lighting and immediately knew that whomever turned the lights on didn't know what the heck they were doing, and with all these kids running around and the noise at a level beyond human comprehension, we were flirting with disaster. I went to the switchboard that controls the lighting and flipped the switches to better illuminate the area. To my shock and dismay, everything went dark, and I mean real dark. No problem click, click, click, and they would be back on. That's the way it used to be. However, I guess sometime within the last fifty-five years, some genius decided to put in those goofy neon lights that take twenty-five minutes to light up. The other playground supervisor went ballistic on me, and I had no defense. I knew she felt bad for yelling because she later came up to me and said, "What the hell did you think you were doing?" Okay, I get it. I screwed up because of modern technology. My intentions were good, but the result was not. The last time I got into this much trouble for touching something I was not supposed to touch was when I was on a date in high school. I guess I should have learned my lesson back then.

As I mentioned, the noise level was so intense and the whizzing by of little bodies that were hard to indentify in the darkness made it impossible to put the blame on those responsible for the chaos. I have never been in a cave inhabited by bats, but I now know what that experience must feel like. You can sense the presence of something possibly not human swarming around you. You know it is there, and you feel defenseless. I tried everything in my power to restore some sort of order. I could feel what it must be like to work on a cattle drive, in the dark. However, the cattle are much quieter.

Oh well, it's been twenty minutes and the kids are lining up to go back to their classes, and the lights are starting to come back on. I survived, and life is good. In the words of Annie, the sun will come out tomorrow. The weather forecast calls for rain tomorrow.

Tomorrow is here, and it is worse than rain. The weather is overcast and barely sprinkling. The decision is to send them outside. The preschool and kindergarten kids made their way out onto the playground with instructions not to touch anything that will get them wet, which is like saying "Here is a candy bar, don't eat it." After a brief game of Simon Says, which no one seemed to understand, the sprinkling decided to become a full-fledged rain. Everyone took off like the running of the bulls in Pamplona, Spain, and made their way to the foyer of the school. Trying to contain the noise level to a low scream was just not possible. With just ten minutes left until recess was over, we separated the two grades and had the kindergarten kids go to the gymnasium. It was then that we took a headcount of the sixteen dampened children and came up with fifteen. Okay, sounds good—nope, this is one of those situations where close isn't good enough; we need sixteen. I knew that I must have miscounted, so I tried it again. Yep, fifteen. Okay, not good. Let's try this again. Fifteen again. Okay, who is missing? With the help of the little ones, I said, "If you are not here please, raise your hand." This even confused me. One little girl said she didn't see her friend Alexi. I think that the last time I had this much fear go through me was when I was ten years old and my dad installed a window air conditioner above our bathtub and strung a fourteen-foot extension cord over the hot and cold faucets to the medicine cabinet where the outlet was. This was a different kind of fear, but any way you look at it, fear is fear.

After much searching and beads of sweat, we located Alexi. It appears that she took this opportunity to elevate herself one grade level and decided to become a kindergarten student. I don't have a heart condition and I don't take nitro pills, but I think I may start if we have many more situations like this one.

19

Living like a Rock Star

I learned today that being a playground supervisor does not stop at the school. Believe it or not, there is some sort of rock star status associated with my job. For years, I could never quite grasp the attention my wife, Miss Debbie, would get from the students while shopping at the local grocery store or any other such venue in our town. A screech could be heard saying, "There's Miss Debbie! There's Miss Debbie!" Well, today I had my rock star moment. While shopping at our local Dollar Tree discount store, I heard the unmistakable voice of Kenny, who is in the preschool clan. To the amazement of his parents who had no idea of my elevated stature in their son's eyes, he came running over to me like a heat-seeking missile and began to shimmy up my leg as would a koala bear climbing a eucalyptus tree. This put me in the awkward position of attempting to remain paramount in Kenny's eyes and explaining to his parents that I am harmless while trying to shake their son from his intense grasp on my leg.

Kenny's mother's eyes were focused on me, and I could see that "mama bear ready to attack" mode set in motion. As she began to recoil, I said, "I'm the playground supervisor and Miss Debbie's husband. Don't shoot." I quivered. "*Ooookaaaayyy,*" she responded. Well, that bit of a most uncomfortable moment was behind us, and my status began to slowly return to good guy from pervert. Of course at this moment, you begin to extol all the virtues of their son and how he in particular is the best preschool student ever and how proud they must be being his parents, and it is then that they reveal their reason for visiting the store. It seems that when Kenny is good, he gets a star on a sheet of paper that is attached to the refrigerator and after ten stars, he is entitled to go to the dollar store to pick out a reward. The mother confided to me that it takes a long, long time for Kenny to achieve this goal, which kind of is in contrast to the model I was portraying him to be during my interrogation.

Rock stars have multimillion dollars homes, they take trips to Fiji, they drive Jaguars, they eat lobster at the best restaurants in the world, they buy expensive jewelry and clothes, and they have bodyguards. After closely examining my life, it became quite clear to me. I am not a rock star. I am *the* playground supervisor.

20

Secret Agent Man

In my other life, separate and apart from my playground supervisory duties, I am an international covert spy. Well, maybe not international and not so much covert, but I have spied on people in the past. My actual title is private investigator, a job I have done for about ten years. This is something that I can really embellish upon because, after all, it is undercover, and who really knows what I do other than what I choose to tell them? To four- and five-year-old kids, I just became Bond, James Bond. Actually, I am a closer fit to Austin Powers, but they don't have to know that. Yeah Baby. Having this title allows me to brandish a real private investigator badge. Little do they know about those early morning hours perched inside a van in the seediest part of town, and with the fog moving in, I continued to monitor each and every movement of our subject who was unaware of my presence as she exited the home. Then there were the high speed chases keeping up with my target, knowing that danger lurked around every corner. Hour after hour, day turned to night, and night turned back into day, yet

I continued my chase in an effort to satisfy my client's demands. There were the days of scorching heat, and then there were the bitter cold nights. One does not choose your working conditions, they choose you…okay, I'm back.

Today for the first time, I showed that badge to the preschoolers and told them that I was a spy and that it was very important that we keep this just between us and not let anybody else know so as not to destroy my cover. I had everyone's word that it would be kept secret. I am guessing that no more than six minutes later, the fourth graders came running over to see my credentials. This led to the fifth, sixth, seventh, and eighth grade students checking out for themselves a real live spy. Words like *cool*, *awesome*, *amazing*, and *neat* were used—and that was just me describing myself to them. I don't know who the actual mole was who caused my secret identity to become public, but I had an idea. After careful deliberation and the usual questioning of suspects, I was able to deduce that the culprits were…the entire preschool and kindergarten students. I could see a series of whispers circulating around the room as would happen when someone accidentally has their zipper down and doesn't know it. Boy, that's the last time I entrust four- and five-year-olds with sensitive and confidential information.

One boy in particular was extremely interested in my role as spy and wanted to know if I ever had to call 991, to which I replied that I did, but for some reason I can never get anyone to answer. A teacher walking by heard the conversation and suggested that maybe I should try 911 instead. That just shows that there always is a wisenheimer around trying to bring you down in your moment of glory.

I was totally taken by surprise with the revelation of my secret life as a "spy" being exposed. In my wildest imagination, I never thought it would generate this kind of reaction. One girl asked me if what I do is considered stalking. After some considerable thought, I guess in a sense I am a legal stalker licensed by the state. Another fourth grade girl who at first refused to believe my involvement in this underworld activity finally was persuaded by her peers that, in fact, I was a "spy." As I continued to relate some top secret stories with dates and names being changed to protect the innocent, she got this weird look on her face and asked me if I had every spied on her or her family. I assured her that since they were an upstanding and law-abiding family, I have had no reason to spy on them. With much relief in her voice and the color starting to come back to her face, she said, "Good, because sometimes my dad goes to the bathroom outside."

No sooner than having my identity exposed, I was called upon to mediate and investigate an incident on the playground. It appears that Jason, a four-year-old preschool student, was physically attacked by another preschool subject. Showing the signs of a red mark next to his right eye about the size of a flea's bowel movement, it became clear that we must find the perpetrator and bring this case to a close. Luckily, we had an eyewitness, being Jason himself. He immediately accused Eddie as the attacker. Eddie was easily apprehended since the playground area for the preschoolers is approximately twenty feet by twenty feet. It was time to apprehend the suspect and get him to confess. This was going to be a tough one since Eddie denied any wrongdoing. "Come on, Eddie, confess, there is no getting out of this," I said. "The evidence is stacked against you higher than double pancake day at IHOP." Still, he would not budge from his original stance of not guilty. Okay, we have ways to make you talk. Eddie remained adamant in his denial. I guess the thing to do now is to confront the victim and his attacker at the same time. As I brought the two together, I asked Jason to point to the person responsible for the vicious attack. To my total surprise, Jason slowly turned almost 180 degrees and with his finger, he pointed to this sweet, little, innocent girl playing jump rope all by herself and not bothering anyone. "It was her," he said. Let the record show that Jason was pointing to Addie, not Eddie. Okay, it appears we have a case of mistaken identity. Addie eventually admitted to the crime with the defense that it was an accident. Sorry, Eddie. In the words of that great and poignant *Saturday Night Live* skit, it was Emily Litella who said, "Never mind."

Whatever happens, I have now elevated my status in their eyes, and I will remain shrouded in mystery and continue to be shaken not stirred because I am the playground supervisor also known as the Man of Mystery. Danger is my middle name. Well actually it's Charles, but I never liked it.

21

The Most Wonderful Time of the Year

I guess I should give some kind of a timeline as to where I am in this, my first year as playground supervisor. We are about to enter that much anticipated time of year where we prepare our home for that special visitor with much anticipation and anxiety. The lights go up and the decorations are abundant throughout the yard. There is that feeling of crispness in the air as the little ones prepare for that holiday feeling. Yep, it's time for Halloween.

The kids are beginning to reveal their choices of Halloween costumes. I was told by Miss Debbie that it usually is not a good idea to try and guess what they are going to be because if you guess it right, they get mad, and if you don't guess correctly, they still get mad, so it is a no-win situation; however, I still felt I wanted to pursue it. One girl told me of her desire to be a shower curtain. I am trying to wrap my mind around this and figure out the meaning and actual configuration in making this work. On further thought, it occurred to me that this could be the scariest reveal of all time. I have read in the past that Janet

Leigh herself would not wear this kind of attire. I am fairly confident that this six-year-old has never seen the movie *Psycho*. Knowing this little girl's personality after viewing the movie, she would mostly likely be scarred for life and would go back to being a princess or a cowgirl.

Another little girl told me that she was going to be a cupcake. About the only thing scary about that costume is the calories.

As I was tending to the preschoolers getting them settled for lunch, Patrick blurted out to me that Robert, who was sitting right next to him was going to be a ballerina for Halloween. Right away my training told me that this was a situation that could lead to fisticuffs between the two five-year-old youngsters. Back in my day, those were fighting words. I knew this was something that needed to be immediately addressed and defused, so I gave Robert the opportunity to correct this erroneous claim. "Robert, what are you going to be for Halloween?" I said. In that strong confident voice and that sure-of-himself attitude, he said without hesitation, "A ballerina."

Frankly, I am not a big fan of Halloween. I even got to the point where I would answer the door and with a handful of Jolly Ranchers I would reach into their bag with my hand and I would tap the inside of it with my finger, emulating the sound of candy dropping to the bottom when in fact I was retaining the candy grasped in the palm of my hand. This is a great magician trick. It doesn't work real well when your house is the first one that the beggar—I mean, Halloweener comes to visit. Okay, I am not proud of my actions; in fact, I am totally embarrassed and humiliated by them, but in my own defense, they were cutting into my time watching *Wheel of Fortune*. I really don't like being interrupted whenever Vanna turns a consonant or a vowel.

Halloween used to be ghosts and goblins and witches and black cats. To me Halloween has become an excuse for boys to dress like girls and girls to dress like boys, and then there is always Alice, the sixty-six-year-old lady who lives two blocks away and apparently has never gotten the memo that Halloween is like Trix cereal. It's for kids. Every year she shows up in something from her closet with that always charcoal beard. I guess she still has that sweet tooth, but further examination reveals that she may have literally lost that sweet tooth some years ago.

Well, the big anticipated day is finally here. I really don't understand the thinking behind a lot of these costumes. Parents need to know that when they send their kids to school in costumes that totally confine the child's ability to go to the bathroom, a big problem ensues. There are snaps and hooks and hoods and boots that have to be removed in order to get to that point where they can adequately be prepped for the restroom adventure. What should be a three-minute process turns into a ten-minute ordeal. The kids also become the character that they are representing. Superman and Batman have kidneys too, and apparently they are not made of steel. If I decide to do this playground supervisor thing again next year, I think I will call in sick when Halloween arrives.

22

Bundle Up Your Overcoat

Cold weather has started to set in, and with it there are situations that are arising that I did not foresee back in the warmer days. When the kids know they are going outside in colder weather, they come prepared, wearing their coats to the cafeteria. For the older students, it isn't a problem since they take the coat off and put it behind their chair where it is there waiting for them for the duration of the lunch hour. The younger kids seem to have a problem with this. Since it takes them longer to take it off and even longer to put it back on, they prefer to just keep them on. For the few who do take their coat off, it usually ends up on the floor and gets stepped on by passersby, so for the most part, they are worn during lunch. There was a very popular play a few years ago called *Joseph and the Amazing Technicolor Dream Coat* where he had a coat of many colors. After a couple of lunches, the younger students now have coats of many flavors, including chili, applesauce, catsup, mustard, chocolate milk, and the ever popular pickle juice, just to name a few. A Scotch Guard has not been invented to prevent the damage that these kids can inflict on this fabric.

It is also that time of the year where the little ones run around with their coats wide open, even after we have taken the time to zip them up. Another side effect of cooler weather is the snot that runs freely and uninhibited down their noses, but eventually finds its way to the cuff of the jacket. No better starch has ever been manufactured. Besides all this, with today's winter attire, we are also dealing with gloves with fingers, gloves without fingers, scarves, stocking hats with faces on them, as well as Elmer Fudd hunting caps complete with chin strap, coats that zip, coats that button, coats that Velcro, and coats that snap. I am exhausted just thinking about bundling these kids up for the brief stint outside. The best part is that since it takes so long to prepare everyone for the outside venture, we only have a total of three minutes left before recess ends.

With the kids having to go outside, that also means that I have to go outside. I have suddenly developed the no-neck syndrome from having my shoulders clinched to the sides of my ears. I must now rotate my entire body to see what is happening outside the range of my peripheral vision. My walking has been reduced to that similar to a federal prisoner who has been shackled with leg irons. Running to the aid of a fallen student is reminiscent of someone who is holding back that occasional bout of diarrhea, hoping that you will not be late in your dash to the finish line.

The one thing that keeps me going during these cold blustery days is the thought of my hot tub just waiting to warm and massage my aching chilled body. Now if I just had one, that would be great.

23

Gone but Not Forgotten

I ruined my perfect attendance today. A situation came up where we decided to switch our television carriers. I don't wish to dish on anyone, but I feel I must be direct. When you make an appointment and are told that a serviceman will be there between 8:00 a.m. and noon, it is pretty much a given that they will show up much closer to that noon time.

As I sat here waiting for that van to show up, I decided to be productive and put my talents to good use. The first thing that came to mind was to fill that humidifier. It always seems to run dry in the middle of the night, and there is no way I am getting up at that time of the morning to hold the water reservoir under the cold water faucet. I would rather put up with the clogged sinuses and crusty boogers in my nose rather than remedy the situation at 3:00 a.m.

Secondly, I remembered those soap slivers in the shower stall that are too small to do anything with, so I decided to mold them into one big bar. It is not as easy as it sounds since it takes a lot of time to pull off the hairs stuck to them, but the end result is a new bar of soap, sort of.

Thirdly, I wanted to finish that crossword puzzle book that has been difficult for me to complete. I can concentrate a lot better when no one is around because it also allows me the privacy to look in the back of the book and cheat, sort of like golfing by yourself without anyone there with you counting all of your strokes.

Fourthly, today would be the perfect time to call my financial advisor and check on the status of my fortune. I know that the economy has not been doing that well, but I especially did not feel good about things as soon as I identified myself and his response was, "What is your name again?"

Fifthly, I am not sure if *fifthly* is even a word, but anyway you know what I mean. I thought I would be productive despite my wife's pleading not to be and decided to do a load of laundry. She tells me that you are supposed to sort that stuff. Once again germ phobia plays a part in my life. There is no way I am going to touch each and every item in that hamper, so I emptied the hamper directly into the washing machine, poured in the specified dose of laundry detergent, pressed the settings, and went on my merry way. About a half hour later, I returned to find the washer approximately three feet from where I had last seen it, which tells me that I may have slightly overloaded it, causing an unbalance in the machine. After pushing everything back in place, I deposited the items in the dryer. Dryers are pretty easy to operate, but I found out that an overpacked dryer takes a long time to dry things. After things were finally dry, I thought I would go that extra step and fold the laundered towels and clothing. After folding a few items, it appeared that maybe a couple of things might have changed color by a tint or two, but one thing that was quite obvious is that when you wash towels and socks together, you will need to have a lot of spare time ahead of you picking all the lint balls off of your socks. I don't think that Miss Debbie's response is going to be "At least he tried to help."

Sixthly, again maybe not a word, this would be a good time to turn the toaster upside down and shake out all of the excess toast crumbs that fall to the bottom of the toaster. Fortunately by this time, the doorbell rang, and as I answered it, there standing before me is the television hookup guy right on time—noon.

24

New Kid on the Block

As I arrived at the school today and punched in at the time clock, there was some uncertainty as to whether or not we would be going outside for recess. The principal told me that it was pretty definite that we would be staying in today because of misty rain outside. My response was that "misty rain" sounded like an adult film star's name, and if that was the case, we should not subject the kids to that influence; however, I would be willing to go outside and make sure that she vacated the premises no matter how long it would take me to get her to leave. I thought this was pretty funny, but the reaction I got left me once again questioning my ability as a standup comic. Number one rule in standup comedy is to know your audience.

I made my regular rounds around the various tables today, making sure that everyone was having a great day and contributing to small talk. When I got to the third grade table, I told them about my own granddaughter, who was a third grade student in another town. I told them that she should actually be in second grade but was moved up a grade. Little Melissa immediately piped in and told me that was nothing special because their classmate Kyle, who is in their third grade class, should be in fourth grade.

Overall it was a pretty weird day. Once again our little friend Ricky, who seems to be infatuated with the little boys' room, claimed that he had to use the facilities, but not in those exact words. He grabbed himself, winched his eyes, crouched over in a forty-five-degree angle, and said that he had to go. The preschool teacher told me to ignore him because he already has gone several times today and he was playing wolf. Well, to make a long story short, the wolf peed his pants. I thought I smelled the odor of urine earlier as I walked by that area of the lunch room, but I just passed it off as the aroma of the lunch on this particular day. It is obvious to all concerned that when the parents send an extra change of clothes, everybody within earshot pretty much knows what to expect. Several hours later, I still can't get that aroma of denim soaked with urine out of my nose. Ricky continues to be the main reason that I may choose not to return to the lunchroom and playground duties next year.

Speaking of peeing your pants, stick with me on this one. All classes are separated and sit together at their individual tables. This is where an amazing phenomenon takes place. Preschool and kindergarten students sit intermixed without any question, but then we get the segregation ritual where first grade through seventh grade are totally apart from each other, with the girls at one end of the table and the boys at the other end, with at least six chairs in between acting as a barrier. I think, if my memory serves me correctly, this is called the cootie syndrome. I went through it as a rite of passage when I was young, and it is nice to see that it continues on to this day. The eighth grade students break this tradition and sit so close to each other that I am concerned they are going to get blisters on their elbows. Now for the interesting part, the seventh grade boys invaded the seventh grade girls' part of the table today and sat together for the first time this year. What could the reason be? Could it be that the conversation on this particular day was more interesting than other day? No. Could it be that the heat was not working and everyone was trying to get close to stay warm? No. Could it be that there was a new female student who just happened to be pretty cute? Bingo! Pee your pants time. Being the new kid on the block can be very scary and intimidating, but in this girl's case, I think she is going to do just fine. It's the seventh grade boys that I am worried about.

I had a heads-up that there was going to be a new student, so as playground supervisor, I took it upon myself to be a one-person welcoming committee. I knew her name and thought I would surprise her. I approached her and said, "Samantha, glad you are here." Her response to me was, "I go by Sam."

25

Badges, We Don't Need No Stinkin' Badges

Once each year the kitchen in the cafeteria is taken over by the elderly ladies society, which I will refer to as the White-Haired Mafia. They bake something called Rozek pastries. They bake several hundred of these to sell for profit that goes to the needs of the school. This is a very worthwhile project that benefits the school considerably, so you let them have their way knowing ahead of time that it is important to point out that no one is to cross these women in any way. They have been known to attack you with their ladles and spatulas if you cross that boundary. They take total control of the kitchen facilities, which means that the lunch must be altered to accommodate the students.

Today the kids were served sack lunches to replace the normal flow of everyday lunch. This is when total surprise sets in. The kids were totally enthralled by the selection offered to them. Inside the paper bag were the following items: peanut butter sandwich, apple, corn chips, and fruit gummy snacks. Just because there was no tray and silverware and the pattern was altered, you would think that the world's best chef was on the premises. I was able to do a short survey and found out that the junior high students weren't as enthralled with this clever maneuver and questioned the fulfillment of today's menu. This prompted me to tell the students that since the general consensus approved today's change, tomorrow's lunch will also be in a paper bag. We will be having spaghetti, green beans, and applesauce. I told them that they needed to eat fast before the items seeped through the bottom of the bag.

I think I am a pretty likable kind of guy, but there is one person I can't get to like me. She comes three times a week with her mother who helps out in the cafeteria. Her name is Lily, and she is two years old. For the life of me, I have tried to get at least a smile out of her but to no avail. She constantly shakes her head in the no direction on everything I do to get her attention, sort of like the girls in high school used to do when I tried to get their attention back then. Today I asked her if she would like a new car. No. I asked her if she would like a new house. No. When a third grader asked her if she wanted a fruit snack, she immediately shook her head yes. I only hope that her mother does not equip her with a mace.

As I was leaving for the day, the principal presented me with my photo identification card to be worn around my neck each and every day. My first reaction was, "Okay, that's nice." The longer I thought about this, the more confused I became since I have been here for three months. I know everyone there and everyone knows me. Why do I need a picture of myself hung around my neck? Reason number one could be that I am just so darn good-looking and I have it at my immediate beck and call to continue to remind myself. No, I don't think that's it. Reason number two might be in case I am ever arrested, we can save the taxpayers the expense of a mug shot. That's probably not it either. Reason number three is that it will come in handy, because of my age, when I forget who I am. That might be the reason, but probably not. I am thinking that with today's confusing world that is designed to make things upside down from how things used to be, this is just another one of those new protect-your-butt things. As I continue to ponder this new procedure, my past came to mind when things were so much more simplistic. We drank out of a garden hose, we ran with scissors, we left our doors unlocked for most of the day and sometimes at night, we sat two feet from the television. If you got lost, you could ask any stranger for help. We would shop at the local neighborhood grocery store that was about the size of a phone booth. Sorry, I shouldn't have said phone booth since my younger readers won't know what I am talking about. If we didn't have enough money to pay him, he just said to bring it when we had it and take a handful of candy with you when you leave. The list goes on and on.

As a final show of disobedience, I went home and on this thing called a computer, I printed off a photo of George Clooney and taped it over my picture. I await the reaction and my fate when I show up tomorrow with this around my neck.

The reaction was varied. First of all, my adult peers didn't notice since we are all pretty much eye-level with one another, and the photo hangs at mid stomach. The younger ones who are eye level with my navel noticed almost immediately. "Hey, that's not you." However, my day was made when one second grade girl said that I took a bad picture because I look better than that. Take that, George Clooney.

After realizing that no one really knew who George Clooney was, I decided to change the photo to Mickey Mouse. You would have thought that Walt Disney himself walked into that cafeteria. I was the talk of the day, and I don't think that I can top this. It is really going to be a letdown when I decide to go with my real image.

26

An Apple a Day

After three and a half months, it finally happened to me along with all other great writers. I have developed a severe case of writer's block. I am not sure if this is something that is temporary or just a passing phase. Everything that I have written about in this book actually—or should I say, pretty much—happened, and in the beginning, it came in such a rush of episodes. It was probably several rewrites before Mark Twain finally changed Bobby Smith and Jerry Thompson to Tom Sawyer and Huckleberry Finn.

The Bible is another great example of someone having writer's block. If you notice they can go several thousands of years before they pick up on something. It seems there was a lot to write about with so-and-so who begot somebody and another so-and-so begot another somebody, and then when all the begetting was over, things kind of slowed up a little until Moses gave them something to talk about. Then there was that real good chapter on Sodom and Gomorrah, which can really grab your interest. Then about three thousand years later, Jesus came along and all of a sudden there was a whole bunch of new material to write about for some time, but if you notice, they seem to be going through that slow period again since no one has added anything to the Bible in quite some time. I guess they kind of wrote themselves into a corner when they titled it the Old Testament and the New Testament. What will they call the next series, "the Newest of the Testaments" or "Here We Go Again"?

Today in an effort to create something, I told the preschoolers that if you hold an apple in one hand and hold the stem with the other hand and say the alphabet as you turn the apple, your favorite letter will be when the stem falls off. I don't think that I made this up. I recall it from somewhere in my childhood. When the letter H came up, I told the little girl to come up with a word that began with H. Her response was an immediate horse. I came up with happy. She came up with Henry. I came up with hemorrhoids. I think that if Happy Henry the horse had hemorrhoids, he wouldn't be very happy. This prompted every other student to emulate this stupid game. When they could not get the stem to fall off because of lack of strength in their fingers, they insisted that I do if for them. I knew I started something that I could not get out of, so I agreed to help those who were having difficulties, but what I didn't anticipate is when I had to do this to the half-eaten apples. I guess kids don't mind when someone plays with their food before they eat it.

Hey Mister, Can You Tie My Shoes?

Sometimes it takes a child to put things in perspective. Of the sixteen children in the preschool class, there is one girl in particular who is head and shoulders taller and more mature than the other fifteen. This prompted me to go up to her and ask her how old she was. She told me that she was four. I asked her when she was going to be five. In the most honest and clear response that any four year old could say, she said, "On my next birthday."

Today I did something that was probably not very nice, but the end result was achieved. Another lady who helps out during the noon hour told me that one of the second grade boys had gone to the bathroom and it had been ten minutes and he had not come out. She said she called for him but got no response and was getting a little concerned. Bathrooms seem to be a main theme here lately. I went to the bathroom and called his name, but still no response. As I bent down, I could see two little feet dangling inside the stall, so it was obvious that Elvis had not left the building. No matter what I said, he would not respond, so in a last ditch effort I told him that he was missing out because they were giving away free bikes and if he didn't hurry he was not going to get one. Those two little feet hit the floor faster than a traveling salesman getting caught with the farmer's daughter, and he was joining everyone else in just seconds.

In a sense, I was very proud of how I outwitted a second grader, but I had a guilty feeling for the rest of the day, wondering if he met the school's hygienic standards.

27

Teach Your Children Good—I Mean, Well

In an earlier chapter, I mentioned how I used to teach at this school some forty-plus years ago. I guess this somehow qualifies me to be a substitute teacher at this stage of my life. Having just finished three and a half months as playground supervisor, the opportunity presented itself to teach third grade for a day. I was excited at the thought of it and decided to give it a go. The students greeted me with over the top enthusiasm and downright giddiness, which to me was the first clue that I lost control from the start. A seatbelt has not been invented that could keep those kids in their chairs as long as I was in the classroom.

One young boy in particular was having problems with his division on this particular day. The assignment was to work on dividing by six. When it came to twenty-four divided by six, he was developing a brain fart so I decided to come to his rescue. Being out of the realm of teaching for so long, I realize that things are done differently now, so I just had to revert back to my basic thinking. I had him visualize a six-pack of let's say soda pop I then told him to get another six-pack of let's say soda pop and so on and so on until he had twenty-four bottles of let's say soda pop. When there are finally twenty-four bottles of let's say soda pop, how many six-packs are there. After a few agonizing seconds of finger counting, he triumphantly shouted "*Four!*" I counted on my fingers to make sure he was right, and then confirmed his correct answer. "*I get it, I get it!*" he shouted. That old feeling of seeing something click with someone that you were responsible for was overwhelming. This prompted me to urge him to go to the next level of thirty divided by six. After several moments of trying, he said, "I don't get it." I then said, "If you have six bottles of let's say soda pop…"

It was now time to move on to religion, which I must admit is not my best subject to explain to third graders. Wouldn't you know it? Today's assignment we were to work on the Ten Commandments. I can easily explain most of them to the kids, but when we got to "Thou shall not commit adultery" and they wanted an explanation as to what that meant, I found myself to be totally at a loss. This kind of goes along with the one that says we are not to covet thy neighbor's wife. Third graders can be kind of persistent, and it was at this moment when the beads of sweat were starting to form and caused my confident persona to crumble. As I regained my composure and realized that they needed an explanation, I calmly told them to visualize a six-pack of let's say soda pop some candles and a little Dean Martin playing softly in the background.

There is also that commandment that states you should not covet thy neighbor's goods…unless they have a boat.

With the day running down and my debut as substitute teacher coming to an end, I guess I got a little slap happy when one little girl asked for a definition of the word *frankincense*. I knew right away that this was one of those gifts brought by the wise men to baby Jesus along with myrrh and gold. Frankly, if they were baring these gifts to me, I would have regifted the frankincense and myrrh and kept the gold—but that's just me. Getting back to the little girl's question, I knew I had to think fast on my feet so the first thing that came to my mind was that frankincense is the change that Frankenstein carries in his pocket. I thought I would get a big, hearty laugh from this, but they either didn't get it or didn't think it was funny. I finally resorted to what all teachers do when they are presented a question that they have no answer for: go home and look it up.

My day is finally over and physically I feel like I have been run over by a Mac truck. Mentally, I am so exhausted that the thought of just going home and reading the TV guide is enough to make my brain boil. I guess it was all worth it when I was dragging myself to my car and one of the other teachers whose daughter was in my class came up to me to say that her daughter just told her that I was the best substitute teacher *ever*.

28

Intermission

We have reached the halfway point of this project. It is Christmas vacation time, and the kids are gone for seventeen days. I have to admit that the first four months just flew by and provided me a treasure trove of entertaining stories where, in some cases, I just couldn't write fast enough. I am not sure what challenges the kids will unknowingly provide me for the remainder of the school year, but I am sure they will be entertaining.

Just like in the novel *A Christmas Carol*, I also have a past, present, and future to write about. You have already been exposed to what is now the past, and as I write this today, you are reading about the present, so I guess there is only one more ghost to visit you which will take us on our school year journey to the end of May.

In the memorable words of Tiny Tim—no not the tiptoe-through-the tulips-guy, but the kid in Dickens's novel: "God help us everyone," Or something close to that. See you in the New Year.

29

I'm Baaaack, Baby, It's Cold Outside

Here it is, the night before we resume the school schedule after the Christmas break and we received a call saying that there will be no school tomorrow because it is too cold outside. In my day, I don't ever remember school being closed because of it being too cold. There is something today called wind chill. Right now, it is two below zero outside, but we are being told that there is a wind chill making it forty-five below. I think we are raising a generation of sissies. In reality, I am five-feet-eight tall, but in my mind I am six-feet-two tall. As much as I think of myself as six-feet-two tall, I am still five-feet-eight tall—and that is a fact. I cannot grasp today's thinking and find it totally inept. As far as tomorrow…I will stay in bed nice and cozy and sleep in, knowing that I don't have to go out in that ridiculous cold weather.

Boy, it must really be cold outside. We just received another call telling us that we have yet another day to cozy up in bed and stay home because school will be closed yet another day. This sounds really tempting, but I am anxious to get back into a regular routine. Thank goodness that the mail did not come today. I would have had to have gone out and gotten it. What a range of extreme emotions I have been going through. Please let's get going, but don't send me out there. How weird is that?

It has been so long since I have seen the kids at school that I have forgotten most of the names I had memorized.

I am back, and it is as if I have not missed a day. The kids have that overly enthusiastic exuberance that is only present in youth. The teachers on the other hand are displaying a demeanor of someone who has been deprived of all the pleasures of life. It can be really a challenge to restart that inner motor, especially after a nineteen-day shutdown. I was able to recognize the short temperedness in most of the adults and made it a point to avoid eye contact and only speak when spoken to. I think it worked.

Of course, I had to listen to the kids and how exciting their Christmas vacation was. After a while, you just sort of nod your head and act like you are really excited hearing about Santa and all of the neat things that he brought.

A highlight of coming back was finally making the eighth grade students laugh…a little. With it being so cold outside, I told them that on the way to school, I said the words "Global Warming," but they froze before I could get them out. Okay, I had to explain to them that it was an oxymoron of sorts, but before that I had to explain to them what an oxymoron on was. With all this explaining going on, I think the true meaning of the joke was lost somewhere between *Global* and *Warming*. Looking back now, the little chuckles that I got were most likely an attempt to stroke my ego, so I would go away. Laugh or no laugh, it is still so cold outside that even Al Gore was complaining about a major case of shrinkage.

With this new beginning, I decided to take this time and reinvent myself. I grew a beard, had an eye exam, and now wear glasses all the time, and last but not least—through the magic of cosmetic hair restoration—I went from dark brown to pepper gray overnight. In my mind, I felt that the remake was needed and overdue, but it took an e-mail from Stevie Wonder to assure me that I looked pretty good. You can always count on Stevie to tell it like it is.

This first day back was going to be very interesting since kids are known to tell it like it is, but I was prepared for them. The looks on their faces told the whole story. "Hey, you are wearing glasses." "You look different." It took a fifth grade boy to finally come right out and say, "You had dark hair the last time I saw you and now it's gray. What happened?" I was waiting for this response, and with the calmness of a blind lion tamer covered in raw meat, I told him that since I was a spy, I need to change my looks every so often so that I am not recognized by the people whom I am spying on. Not only did this satisfy his curiosity, but it once again elevated me to that super star status that all playground supervisors seek. Walking around the cafeteria,

I could feel the whispers and hear the eyes centered on me as I continued on with my coming out ceremony. I wondered how long the attention would last and when would I be able to settle back in to my role as elementary recreational supervisor. Would I now have to live my life in the spotlight, never being able to settle back and enjoy the low profile that I had always enjoyed? Would the glare of the paparazzi be more than I could handle? It wasn't long before I got the answer I was looking for. Within a matter of four minutes, everything went back to the way it had been. The kids really didn't give a crap.

As I was walking around, one young preschooler grabbed my attention and proceeded to tell me that he and his dad were building a space ship in their garage for the purpose of traveling into outer space. He said that he wanted to bring an alien back. He thought that the big aliens might be mean, so he would be bringing back a kid alien. In his generosity, he offered to take any of his classmates with him. One little girl in particular expressed a deep desire to go on this venture. After listening to her pleas for acceptance, I asked her if she was aware that she would need a space suit. She said she never thought of that, but she would get her dad to buy her one. I am not sure if this space ship project will be completed by the end of the school year since they are only at the installing of the rockets part, but in the event that it is, you are in for a very interesting chapter yet to come.

Ah, back to the fascinating to the absurd. There is never a dull moment when you are dealing with kids and their imaginations.

We just finished a three-day holiday, being off Monday because of Martin Luther King's birthday. I know that technology is moving at a rapid pace, but in my wildest imagination, I never thought that our preschool student with the space ship would be able to accomplish his goal of space travel in such a short time. I was told today that over the weekend, he went to the moon. He met an alien there that he described as fat and ugly. I asked him what the alien had to say, and he told me that there were a lot of bad words so he couldn't repeat what he said. He said that he traveled at night. I asked him how long it took him to get there, and he said about forty-five minutes. He said that it took about the same amount of time to get back. He went at night time because he wasn't scared. When I asked him what he took to eat on the venture, he said that he took some cheese cake and some other stuff that belonged to his dad, but he didn't mind.

At this time, I am either dealing with someone who is bordering on possible genius mentality or someone who as the janitor described as, "Close to the dark side." Whatever the case, it is a totally entertaining story related in such a sincere way. They called Edison a nut case.

30

They Call Me Mellow Jell-o

I am not sure if education is always a good thing. Today we had Jell-o as one of our side dishes along with corn dogs. The kids for the most part really like Jell-o. A few weeks ago, out of my own curiosity, I decided to look up on the internet and find out the origins of Jell-o and how it came to be. It just seemed to me that this is really some kind of weird stuff. As it turns out, Jell-o, which is a brand name like Band-Aid is to adhesive bandages, is actually a gelatin made from a processed version of a structural protein called collagen that is found in many animals, including humans. Collagen is a fibrous protein that strengthens the body's connective tissues and allows them to be elastic and stretch without breaking. Collagen can come from cow or pig bones, hides, and connective tissues. Collagen doesn't dissolve in water in its natural form. Manufacturers grind the body parts and treat them with a strong acid and a strong base to dissolve the collagen. Then the pretreated material is boiled. The protein ends up being partially broken down, and the resulting product is a gelatin solution. The solution is chilled into a jelly-like material, cut, and dried in a special chamber. At this point, the dried gelatin is ground into a fine powder. I told the cooks about my recent discovery and was surprised to find out that they already knew of this amazing transformation. I guess that this is part of their training. I then proceeded to tell them that this would be something really interesting and educational for the kids, and I was going to go tell them. It was then I was greeted with a definitive and resounding *No!*

Okay, I kept my promise, except for one seventh grade girl who didn't like Jell-o in the first place. I proceeded to tell her the Jell-o story, and I could see the horror engulf her eyes. She continued to deny my claims until finally the image of boiled bones and tendons drenched her imagination. As is usually the case, in order to spread the word you can telegraph, telephone, or tell a woman, and you can be assured that the message will get around. Okay, I know that was a sexist remark, but to say "tell a man" just doesn't sound right. Anyway, the word traveled through the seventh grade faster than a drunken Justin Bieber in a Lamborghini. The general consensus was that I was probably not telling the truth. The words I left them with were, "Look it up."

Again, reverse global warming raised its ugly head. There were two more days of no school due to the extreme cold conditions. This gave me a great opportunity to go to the grocery store, do the banking, walk five miles at the local armory, and visit the in-laws. Do you see the irony here? It is too cold to have school, and we are told by people in the media, who made it to work, to stay in the house. I don't get it. According to the powers that be, we only have one more day on the school calendar allowed for emergency days. After that we will have to make them up by extending the school year into June. My pool will be open by then, and I am not a big fan of continuing this playground duty into my lounging time, but by the way this goofy climate has gone, I may still be thawing out the pool water.

31

This Is The Week That Was

This week is Catholic Schools Week, and each day is filled with child and parent activities. There is a spaghetti dinner, a talent show, a parents-come-to-lunch day, a movie and popcorn activity, a book sale, and anything else you can think of to involve the parents. This also gives me a great opportunity to size up the kids with the people who created them.

I was able to track down the parents of the boy who went to the moon and back. Just as I thought, they were not aware of his venture and did not observe any missing food in the pantry. I think I may have gotten our space traveler in a little trouble with his parents since they were not aware of his extraterrestrial exploits and apparently have a rule that he is not allowed to cross the street without their assistance. Since he got back safely, I think they will overlook his travels and look with pride on his accomplishment. Not too many preschoolers can say they went to the moon and back. On second thought, I think most of them have claimed that they have but that doesn't lessen the feat.

Hey Mister, Can You Tie My Shoes?

This day and age brings many new challenges that can cause a moment of awkwardness. Little Sophia introduced me to her mother, a nice, pleasant-looking woman probably in her thirties. In an effort to be polite, I went on a long rant on what a great child she had and how it was a pleasure to be a playground supervisor in charge of such a wonder girl and how she has made my job so much easier. While waiting for some sort of reply—like maybe, thank you—Sophia chimed in that her mother did not speak English. It is times like this that a smile and a nod of the head is all that is needed. I trust that Sophia would then translate to her mother what I said and that I was her favorite playground supervisor and not some sort of dork. Since I don't speak Spanish, I can only hope she was kind to me. How do you say dork in Spanish?

Of course, like any other school, you have the moms, the dads, the stepmoms, the stepdads, the grandparents, the step grandparents, and any other step this and that. It is really a tribute to the children when you see all forms of parents sitting together at the same table conversing and interacting without it resulting in a food fight.

Today's talent show featured dancers, magicians, singers, guitar players, and acrobats. I don't believe I have ever been to a live entertainment show where there has not been some sort of an electronic malfunction. It is comforting to know that things don't always work for other people as well as me. Although *America's Got Talent* may be a few centuries away for these performers, just getting up and performing in front of hundreds of starring eyes can be intimidating, so the effort was appreciated by all.

32

Let It Be

In the course of a long school year, especially with the brutal, long, cold winter that we have had, tempers can run at a fever pitch, as was proven today at noon hour. I witnessed a second grade girl lying on the gym floor in a fetal position crying as if she had been the victim of a laser happy assailant. The pain was evident to anyone observing the moment. I immediately attended to the situation, only to find out that she was unhappy because Mary Jo did not want to be her friend anymore. Upon further investigation, it was determined that Mary Jo was not only her former friend but also her cousin. As I attempted to defuse the situation and find out the facts of the relationship, I tried to get them to see the potential for a very uncomfortable family reunion, which would most likely be in the coming weeks. When my pleading for reconciliation failed, I reminded them of the eleventh Commandment which says, "Thou shall like thy cousin." Apparently, they are advanced enough in their religion class to know that there are only Ten Commandments. After much coaxing and pleading for the relationship to be saved, I was transfixed to the words of those great mopped-headed musicians from Liverpool. I guess I was not a bit surprised by the girl's unfamiliarity with the ballad makers called the Beatles. I then sang in my familiar off-key and pitchy voice the lyrics, "We can work it out. Life is very short and there's no time for fussing and fighting my friend. Try to see it my way only time will tell if I am right or I am wrong." And so on and so on. What I didn't tell the girls is that the Beatles continued to disagree and never really worked out their differences, which eventually led to the song, "Let It Be."

I walked away feeling a tremendous sense of failure, knowing that my attempts to intervene and save this relationship had fallen on deaf ears. The disappointment I was feeling was indescribable. Not only had I failed to save a friendship, but I could not keep these two families from drifting apart due to the discord between the two combative young ladies.

As I prepared to leave the gymnasium with my head bowed in defeat, I took one last look back, only to see the two friends/cousins with arms around each other singing "We can work it out." I succeeded. If only I could have intervened back in 1970 when the Beatles were having their disagreements, who knows what my influence could have achieved?

33

Top of the Heap

With winter having its grasp on us, the flu season is also here. It is at this time that the creepy crud has taken its toll on several students as well as teachers. I received a call to step in and once again offer my services as substitute since the second grade teacher had been infected with symptoms that are too violent to put into words. All I know is that it involves a toilet and some sort of a bucket to be used simultaneously. Teaching is something I really enjoy doing, but knowing that I am stepping into a germ infected warfare zone can be quite daunting.

My assignment was to oversee the second grade along with an aide who fortunately had everything under control. The day went very smoothly without any hitches. I read some sort of story about a penguin who ran away from home and was eaten by a whale. It would have been nice to be able to prescreen the book for violence but there was no time for that, so we had to settle for the unhappy ending. Then there was the making of the Valentine cards. It is amazing how a five-minute project can take two hours to complete. There is the cutting out of the heart pattern and then the pasting down of the lace fabric. The teacher gives the students instructions regarding the glue, telling them that a dot is a lot. My job is to make the rounds to each individual student and praise their work no matter how badly the cutting job was, and to tell them how lucky their parents are to be the recipients of this beautiful item. It is amazing how far a little dishonesty can go in building a young one's self-esteem. This teaching thing is not too bad. However, as the day progressed, I was informed that the eighth grade teacher would not be assuming her duties the following day, and that my services would once again be needed. Wait a minute, did she say eighth grade? Oh no, not the eighth grade. These are those sneaky, conniving, manipulative teenage people with a hidden agenda. Could I possibly fend off an entire class of these adolescents for an entire school day? I have never placed myself in a situation of authority where everyone was bigger than me. This was going to be interesting.

I called my buddy in Florida, who is a teacher, to ask for some tips to be able to stay in control and not find myself on the defense all day long. He was very helpful in providing me with some corporate team-building projects that are designed with the purpose of diverting the attention of the aggressors. Would this be enough to hold them off for an entire day? To make things worse, this just happened to be Valentine's Day, so the presence of sugar-infested candy would be abundant throughout the school. It was obvious to me that the kids would be bouncing off the walls like a pinball machine from their sugar high.

As I waited for the ringing of the attendance bell, my heart was rapidly beating from anticipation, wondering if I was wise to take on this challenge. There was no turning back. I was the playground supervisor turned eighth grade substitute teacher. My reputation was at stake. You hear people say that they are not quitters; however, I don't subscribe to that policy. I don't think it is a bad thing to be a quitter. If you are a member of a gang about to rob a bank, I think that would be a good time to be a quitter. It is also a good idea to be a quitter when playing golf and that electrical storm is about ready to hit. I have been known to quit at times when the going got tough, especially when it comes to computers and technology and trying to sort things out when they are not going so smoothly, but I was not going to quit this time.

My first goal was to let them know that I knew that they knew that I knew that they knew that…well, you get the point.

After the initial shock wore off, it became clear to me that when you step in as a substitute teacher, it is pretty much the same as when a grandparent steps in to watch the grandkids. All of the normal rules kind of go out the window, and it is time to spoil the kids. As it turned out, the eighth graders are really a nice bunch of young adults. Their questions were involved and insightful, and it turned out to be a rewarding experience for me. I was really surprised to find out that they actually speak English and have a pretty good grasp on social mores and traditions.

I got through the day like a lion tamer would get through his act, keep them satisfied and content so that the attack mode does not kick in. I thought that since I had broken the barrier and for a short time was part of their world, I would be able to be accepted into their inner circle. This was not the case. The next lunch period proved to be just like all the rest. The eighth graders were once again aloof and standoffish toward the playground supervisor. At first, I was taken back and resentful that I had not been accepted into their society, but you could feel that the iron curtain had been opened just a little bit, and I was allowed to be part of their world for a short time. You need to understand that they are eighth graders; they are king of the hill, top of the heap, a number one, top of the list, and if they can make it here, they can make it anywhere. Gee, I bet if you put some music to that, you could have a pretty good song.

I survived with my reputation as cool guy intact. I definitely would do it again, but I am not going to sabotage anyone to get there. Just knowing that I walked into the pit of fire and came out stronger than when I went in is something to be proud of. I did it.

34

Stop the World, I Want to Get Off

This book or collection of experiences has been an attempt to show the humorous side of being a cafeteria and playground supervisor. Lately there has been nothing funny to write about. The weather has refused to release its grip on us. We are one day away from the first of March, and once again we are looking at subzero temperatures and an oncoming snowstorm expected to dump a possible nine inches of snow on top of the mounds of unthawed ice from previous plowing that has now turned into a disgusting shade of brown and charcoal-gray along with an occasional yellow splattering donated from the neighboring dog. Boy, that was a long sentence, but nowhere near as long as this crazy winter.

As of right now, my morale is low, and my liquor bill is high. Once where there were tan lines around my waist, there is now a deep underwear elastic imprint. The hair on my legs has worn away from constantly wearing socks. My buttocks has been clinched together so hard for so long that my navel has gone from an "inny" to an "outy." My garage looks like a mighty glacier exploded, leaving tons of ice debris too heavy to move without having to rent an end loader. Do you get the point? I am ready to wave the white flag and surrender to mother nature.

Ironically, the kids are performing a play for the public this weekend called *Annie*. They have been preparing for this production for almost the entire school year, and they are now about to learn that it is very possible that the sun will not come out tomorrow. You can bet your bottom dollar that tomorrow there'll be snow and ice and bitter cold. When I'm stuck with a day that's grey and lonely, I just stick up my chin and grin and say, "Well, you don't really want to know what I am thinking of saying. Tomorrow, you're only a day away, and it looks like more of the same depressing crap." They say we have the options of seeing a glass as half-empty or half-full. To me, any which way you look at it, whatever is in that half-full or half-empty glass is frozen, so take that and put it in your pipe and smoke it.

As I reread the last couple of paragraphs, I came to the conclusion that maybe it came off a little bit bitter. You're darn right it is bitter, but not as bitter as this crazy weather. To make matters worse, the principal decided that eleven degrees is warm enough to go outside. What else is there for me to do when 144 children go running outside and I am in charge of their wellbeing? After twenty-five minutes, which seemed more like four hours, we reentered the building. As the kindergarten teacher did her head count, she came up one short. Fortunately, I was aware that the child had asked for permission to go to the bathroom, which was an obvious strategic ploy to get out of this torturous arctic environment. Not a bad idea for a kindergartener. I told her that I guess we must have lost one, but if you do the math, losing just one over the course of a year is really not a very bad average. I could then see what little coloring she had left for her winter complexion was beginning to turn albino-white, so I quickly informed her that the child in question was on his way from the bathroom. I have found that kindergarten teachers don't have much of a sense of humor after dealing with these small ones every day.

I guess the cold brought out the orneriness in me, and I felt that another evil deed was needed. It was time for payback. I proceeded to the office and told the principal that the girl with the lead in tonight's performance of *Annie* had just developed a severe case of laryngitis from being outside in the cold. It made all of the outdoor suffering worthwhile just to see the facial reaction from her, and her mind calculating what the impact of losing your lead star in the play would have. Revenge can be a very rewarding emotion.

Like they say, whoever "they" is, someday, we will look back at this vicious winter and laugh, but for now I don't find anything humorous about it, and that is all I am going to say about that.

35

State Your Name

Seven o'clock on a Monday morning, and the phone rings. Apparently the eighth grade teacher was not going to make it in and would I, could I possibly come in to substitute in such short notice. Being totally unprepared can be quite scary, but I really can't say no, so of course I would be happy to substitute.

The first subject was civics and the studying of the state constitution. Thank God for the answer guide. I like to rely on the smartest kid in the class for the correct answer, just in case I steer myself into a brick wall and become totally unaware of being able to sound authoritative. On this particular day, I guess Monday morning numbness set it, and as I was searching for that magic moment in learning, I came across what sounded like a good idea. Within the learning guide was the state capitol and below that was a phone number. I thought it would be a great idea to call that number to see what was on the other end. The students were taken by surprise at this spur-of-the-moment decision. Of course, with my years of experiencing life, I knew that it would lead to an answering machine, and then I could wrap up the learning session and that would be that. No! Who would have guessed that a real person would be on the other end of this spontaneous phone call? Panic spread across my body faster than a three-year-old's projectile vomit. What was I going to say? Was the call being traced? Would the FBI have direct access to incoming calls for monitoring purposes? What business or agency has real people answering their phones in this day and age of computers and modern technology? A sweet woman on the other side pleasantly said, "Hello, you have reached the state capitol. How can I help you?" Okay, I was in too deep now, so I said the first thing that came to my mind: "Hi." I calmly told her that I was in the process of teaching an eighth grade civics class and we were curious as to the phone number and where it would lead. She asked me if I would like to be connected to anyone within the capitol. I figured that the way the day was going I just possibly could find myself talking to the governor, and since he happens to be on the other side of my political persuasion, it was probably wise to just thank the lady on the other end of the phone and end my conversation with her. The kids were blown away by this simple act of temporary insanity. To them, I was that gutsy substitute teacher for the day who kept them riveted to their seats for a minute or two. To me, I was that trembling temporary educator who could have ended up on the state's most-wanted list had the wrong words come out of my half-comatose body. I used to get sweaty palms just calling the movie phone hotline or the bank for time and temperature. As word spread throughout the school as to the civics lesson and "the phone call," I was told that the principal was so impressed by my hands-on teaching and that I qualified for an A for the day.

With the regular teacher back in place the next day and my normal cafeteria and playground duties restored, I asked her as I was ready to exit the building and head home for my afternoon nap, I mean lunch, what the kids were being taught this afternoon. She said they were studying the skeletal system but that I should have been there when the subject was the digestive system and she had to explain the bowel and anus. For some reason, kids find the anus pretty funny. Wait until they have to go get that colonoscopy for the first time. Let's see how funny they think it is then. If you want to get technical, farts are funny though. I only hope I don't have to sub the day they have to learn about the reproductive system. I don't feel qualified to teach them how certain things south of the border can become such close friends without having a passport. I'm just saying.

36

Time Travelers

The month of March has proven to be one of sickness for several of the teachers on staff. I was once again asked to come forward and provide guidance and instruction to the future leaders of our country. Over a two-week period, I stepped in as substitute teacher for eight out of ten days, which proved to be just one day short of a nervous breakdown.

I always try to keep things fresh and interesting while always putting a different twist on learning. On one particular day with the eighth graders, I decided to become inventive and go back in time. In a Catholic school, it is not unusual to teach religion on a regular basis. Previous attempts at teaching religion have proven to be very challenging for me when it came to religious instruction; however, I decided to give it another whirl. I came up with a concept of going back in time to the biblical era and interview the students as characters from the Bible. I did not anticipate some of the reactions that I got from the kids.

The first attempt of interviewing took me to John the Baptist. I began my questioning by asking the student, who has now assumed the persona of John, by asking what his relationship with Jesus was like when they were kids growing up together. I was not the least bit prepared for the answer I was about to get. Without the least bit of delay, the student responded by saying that they always enjoyed a good competitive game of dodge rock. The visual of two young kids avoiding the hurling of rocks back and forth took me by such surprise that I almost reverted back to the future where I would not have been able to continue interviewing the Bible people. The student proved to be very knowledgeable in his portrayal of John the Baptist. He went on to tell me how he was later beheaded for his preaching, which turned out not to be a very good day for him. I knew at this point that I was outmatched and decided to go on with my time travels adventures and interview another subject.

My next encounter turned out to be Eve, where I found her wandering about, still looking for that Garden of Eden. The girl I selected for this part was a little less familiar with the subject but no less witty. I proceeded to ask her about her relationship with her husband, Adam. She said he was a pretty good husband but immediately scolded me that I was not to appoint any other boy in the class as the Adam portrayer. Okay, I get it. My next question was asking her about her two boys. I asked what their names were. I could see that glassy look come across her face and the obvious I-don't-know look. When I thought I should let her off the hook, she thoughtfully responded, "I really don't remember. It was so long ago." Good answer under the circumstances. I was anxious to follow up, so I told her that I knew that her son Cain killed Abel and what did she think of that. Her response to me was that boys will be boys. I am really outmatched with this class.

My next student, who was known for not being up on things as well as others, assumed the character of Pontius Pilot. I asked him why he did not execute his authority as judge and free Jesus rather than having him crucified. His response was that he would have lost his job and had to go along with it. I thought that this was a very insightful answer from a student who has a hard time staying awake, let alone paying attention. My final question to him was if he would make the same decision if he had it to do over. His answer surprised me, but his explanation shocked me even more. He said I would do the same thing all over again. "Why?" I asked. His reason was that things were meant to be this way, and we wouldn't be talking about this if he was to make a different decision. I was totally taken aback and set on my heels by a student who struggles with about everything that involves academics.

The rest of the characters included Mary, Peter, Mary Magdalene, the three wise men (whom I gave to the class troublemakers and referred to them as the three wise guys), the Roman guards, etc, etc, etc. The venture took the entire class time, and we were fortunate to return to the present day, but our time in the past proved to be not only a learning experience for the kids but for me also.

My four days with the junior high students was very rewarding but extremely exhausting. Just when I thought that I was free to resume my stagnant existence, I was called upon to substitute for the first grade. Going from eighth grade to first grade is equivalent to spending an hour in a sauna and then submerging yourself in ice water. The shock is painful. My observations with the little ones are: 1. Why have the desks not been bolted to the floor? 2. When given ten minutes to answer five questions, why is there that one student who sits staring at the ceiling? When confronted, as time was running out, about his lackadaisical demeanor, his response was, "I haven't gotten that far yet." 3. I am ready to propose that seatbelts be installed on each first grade chair. 4. Pencils break way too easily, and the pencil sharpener never works correctly. There is always that side of the lead where the wood doesn't get shaved away. 5. There is always that student who must raise and wave their hand with such ferocity that you are sure an aneurism is about to develop. When your question is, "How many minutes are there in an hour?" and you finally call on this overreaching student only to get the response: "We made popcorn last night." 6. How can one student eat so many boogers and still be hungry for lunch. 7. How can a first grader possibly spell the word *turn* as *turd*? 8. How can the teacher continue with a straight face?

The one thing I was able to get the students to do was learn how to spell the word *phlegm*. This is what their absent teacher was dealing with. The word is not even close to the level they are learning, but there is something about the difficulty of that word that makes it fun to learn as well as the definition.

The school has implemented a program where outside individuals can donate money to supplement the tuition for students who can use the financial assistance. It is called Adopt a Student. After spending several days with these kids, there are a couple whom I would like to put up for adoption.

At the end of my last day, I guess I was feeling a little bit ornery and cranky and refused to help Tina on her simple request. She asked for my help in removing an earring that she felt was causing some discomfort to her red and puffy pus-filled earlobe. I think I know how to remove an earring from a pierced ear, even though I can positively say that I have never done it. My response to her was that the last time I did something like that, the girl's ear came off in my hand and I haven't done anything like that since. She abruptly backed away and said she would ask someone else. I figured that since there were only a couple of minutes until the final bell, she would be able to have her mom do it well before gangrene would set in.

Somewhere it is written that all things must come to an end. I finished my substitute teaching duties and was instrumental in "no student left behind," except for that one who didn't get inside quickly enough before we locked the doors. Now in the comfort of my quiet and serene existence behind my closed doors with my thoughts reserved just for me, I received that cringing text: Are you available to substitute next Monday, Tuesday, and Thursday?

37

Good-bye, Quincy

I started this project of documenting the goings-on and my actual experience as a noon hour supervisor with as much anxiousness and trepidation as a first-time colonoscopy recipient. I did not know what to expect, nor did I anticipate any positive or negative reactions as the year progressed. We now have a little more than six weeks remaining, and my observations reveal that we have lost the eighth grade as their minds are now absorbing the reality that they will be moving on to bigger and better things. Straight-A students are now bordering on that A minus B plus area. The students who regularly receive the lower end of the grading spectrum are, as you would guess, still receiving the lower end of the grading scale.

Today in the cafeteria, I noticed that the preschool boys are showing a growing affection to the eighth grade girls and are not shy in voicing their desire for the older girls to know it. Loud shouts can be heard across the room, which indicates a male attraction to the opposite sex. When they are successful in getting the female of the species' attention, it is greeted with laughter. In my day, laughter usually meant that I had failed in the ritual of strutting my stuff and I was sent home, head bowed, and needed to lick my wounds, hoping to heal and be ready to fight another day. Not so with these boys. They are encouraged by the female response and become even more embolden and aggressive. As I try to control the situation, I went over to the boy who was obviously the leader of the aggressive pact and proceeded to tell him that girls are bad news, and they will someday cost you a lot of money. I thought that my logic was forceful and would be a positive point for the young male to learn by and save him from much disappointment in the future. In what was probably by far the loudest voice in the cafeteria, he mightily yelled, "They don't cost a lot, they are cheap!"

Throughout the course of the year, several preschool and kindergarten students have received discipline in the form of a five-minute timeout. This involves standing against the building until the punishment has been served. Lately, I have noticed that the occasional offenders have been serving their sentence on a more frequent interval. Some of the reasons for this punishment have included not helping to pick up the mess, not cooperating with others, being overly temperamental, and, oh yeah, trying to bite the head off of a Jesus statue.

On one particular day after serving his sentence of five minutes, Jordan decided to ask for permission to extend his punishment for an additional five minutes. I was totally taken back by his request, but it sounded reasonable to me, so I told him to knock himself out. When the teachers came out to take the children back to their classes, Jordan was seen crying uncontrollably while still standing against the wall. The teacher asked him what the problem was. He immediately told her that I had not been timing him, and he was very unhappy about that. Now we either have a case of a child who feels that he needs additional punishment, or he just pulled a reverse child psychology on us. Whatever the case, I went away scratching my head in wonder, and not sure what other ploys he will develop and use against me.

Being a playground supervisor is not all glitz and glamour as most people would think. In fact, believe it or not, there is no glamour to it at all. Last official account showed 327 shoes tied, 295 coats zipped up, 705 eyes dried due to some sort of tragedy or another, 512 they won't be my friend conversations, and one wiped nose. The wiped nose was by accident. I was bumped into by a first grader with a runny nostril. That turned out to be one less shirt that I now have in my wardrobe. Through it all, I have continued to be there with a smile and ready to convince them that being a playground supervisor is the best one-hour-a-day job in the world.

A moment on the playground today reinforced my opinion on what a great job this actually is. I was asked by the third grade girls to attend a memorial service for

Quincy out by the trash receptacles. Now I must admit that I have never had a personal or even casual relationship with Quincy. I don't even know who Quincy is, but being the caring and concerned guy that I am, I decided to attend the services. As it turned out, Quincy is a small, one-inch piece of rubber figure that obviously had seen better days. I could see the humor in this somewhat morbid ritual and decided to play along. I asked if I could say a few words on Quincy's behalf. I began by praising Quincy and saying that he was a brave soul who would always stand up for himself as well as others, even though he had no feet. I reminisced about how he was denied entry into the Blue Man Group simply because he was purple. With Quincy's head hanging at a right angle, I reminded the group that Quincy always had a good head on his shoulders, even though in his present state, you couldn't tell it. As Quincy was about to pass on to his next life, I surmised that he was important to probably many people over his short life, and even though not being human he was brought into this world from someone's latex.

Okay, the services are now completed, and everyone had their last chance to say their good-byes. The fake tears were a little more than I could handle, but we proceeded with as little fanfare as possible and deposited Quincy into the waste management container. You could hear the small creature rumbling to the bottom, hitting each piece of applesauce, mustard, catsup, and countless other mushy and smelly substances where he finally hit bottom as to what would be his ride to the local landfill. Quincy had been laid to rest. As I walked away knowing that I had done my part in this touching service, one of the third grade girls came running over to me to say, "Quincy is in the garbage can. You got to get him!" "I don't think so."

38

Not the End, Just the Beginning

Now that the end of my nine month journey is approaching, it has struck me that this odyssey has been the equivalent to having a baby. First, there is that twinkle in your eye that says maybe this would be a good time to begin this new venture that will have a tremendous impact on your life. Then there is the realization that you have started something that you must see through. For the first three months, there is that nauseous feeling, making you question your decision of having done this. After some time, it wears off and things go pretty smoothly with an occasional hitch here and there. People can see the transformation in you and are always asking you, "How are things going?" You want to be polite through the mood swings, but there are some days when you just don't want to talk about it. You experience a change of clothing as the nine months pass, and you eagerly cannot wait to once again wear the apparel that you used to wear when this time began nine months ago. As the end of the term nears, you have that feeling of excitement along with a nervous anticipation, wondering if it will be painful. Will

there be a postpartum depression that will set in, knowing that the nine months have come and gone, and you are no longer the same person who you were when this all started. However, this is where the comparison ends. I will be able to walk away from this experiment, knowing there will be no diapers to change, no 2 a.m. feedings, no uncontrollable crying to try to subdue, and no investment of money over the remaining days of my life.

After revealing my thoughts to several of the female teachers about my pregnancy and playground analogy, I came away feeling that they would rather have experienced birth than relive the last nine months.

In hindsight, it was a very enjoyable year that provided me with a lifetime of stories and humorous happenings. It will be very interesting watching these kids grow and mature and turn into prosperous and successful young adults. So as I come to an end of this my last chapter, I can walk away knowing that I did my job and I did it well. There will be 144 students who, when meeting me in the future will say, "There goes the playground supervisor, the guy who made me what I am today."